"Show me a little emotion, Maura."

Her nerves felt coiled tight as a spring. She let the silence grow, and after a while it was no longer threatening.

Xan caressed the curve of her lower lip with a lazy fingertip, imprisoning her eyes with his. Her lips parted reluctantly before his finger tentatively touched the tip of her tongue. Maura savored the taste of him, feeling the heat of her arousal spreading through her body in widening ripples.

After a moment he continued the tracing of her features with his finger, bringing into being a yearning so strong that it became a growing, aching need. Maura closed her eyes for a moment, wanting to erase that need, and when she opened them he had narrowed the space between them and his lips were closing in on hers.

ABOUT THE AUTHOR

Pamela Browning is a former newspaper
columnist, reporter and feature writer who
began writing fiction when her children were
small. As a free-lancer, she has written stories
and articles for local, regional and national
publications. She is also well-known for her
young adult romances, written under the
names Pam Ketter and Melanie Rowe. Pam
makes her home in South Carolina with her
husband, son and daughter.

Books by Pamela Browning

HARLEQUIN AMERICAN ROMANCE

101—CHERISHED BEGINNINGS

HARLEQUIN ROMANCE

2659—TOUCH OF GOLD

These books may be available at your local bookseller.

Don't miss any of our special offers. Write to us at the
following address for information on our newest releases.

Harlequin Reader Service
P.O. Box 52040, Phoenix, AZ 85072-2040
Canadian address: P.O. Box 2800, Postal Station A,
5170 Yonge St., Willowdale, Ont. M2N 6J3

Cherished Beginnings
PAMELA BROWNING

Harlequin Books

TORONTO • NEW YORK • LONDON
AMSTERDAM • PARIS • SYDNEY • HAMBURG
STOCKHOLM • ATHENS • TOKYO • MILAN

Published May 1985
First printing March 1985

ISBN 0-373-16101-8

Printed in Canada

Chapter One

Maura McNeill left her peeling old van in the parking lot of Quinby Hospital and hurried across the street, her borrowed mid-high heels embossing little half-circle marks in the oozing hot asphalt. She shook her auburn hair back from her face and hesitated for a moment in front of the red-brick office building to read the sign on the door.

"Alexander Copeland, M.D., Obstetrics and Gynecology," she said under her breath. Well, she had found his office, all right. Her sense of navigation wasn't bad for a newcomer to the area; she was learning to get around this section of coastal South Carolina, and she could easily have lost her way in the confusing maze of country roads. The fact that she hadn't was proof of her settling in, a thought that pleased her. Whatever the problems and whatever the risks, Maura McNeill had made up her mind that she was in Shuffletown to stay.

Maura elbowed the office door open with a determined push and murmured her name to the receptionist behind the desk before selecting a comfortable chair. She picked up a magazine and looked around with veiled curiosity at her companions in the waiting room.

Half a dozen women in various stages of pregnancy awaited their turns with Dr. Copeland. Maura fit in so well in age and type that anyone would think she was one of those mothers-to-be. But she wasn't.

It was blessedly cool in the doctor's waiting room, a welcome haven from the oppressive heat and humidity outside. Overhead, a ceiling fan circulated the air-conditioned air in breezy silence, its rhythm inducing a kind of drowsiness to the room's occupants. Except for the insistent ripple of music from the speaker mounted on the wall and the occasional swish of a magazine page, the room was quiet.

Maura gazed with detached professional interest at the high rounded abdomen of the pretty, brunette and hugely pregnant young matron who spread uncomfortably into all the corners of the chair across from her.

She'd be eight months along, maybe eight and a half, Maura figured from the look of her. And she could have benefited from a good daily exercise program started earlier in her pregnancy.

"This is my first," volunteered the woman with a shy but understanding smile, mistaking Maura's professional assessment for a more personal one. "How about you?" She looked pointedly and with interest at Maura's flat stomach.

Maura's eyes flew involuntarily to her own left hand,

automatically assuming that the woman thought she was married. A sudden stab of sadness knifed through her at the sight of the ringless finger. She still wasn't used to going without the slender band of white gold she'd worn for the past ten years.

"I'm sorry," said the brunette quickly, noting Maura's hesitation and attributing it to Maura's apparently unwed state. "It's none of my business." Embarrassed, she lifted the magazine she had been reading and hid her flushed cheeks behind it.

"No, it's all right," said Maura warmly, wanting to put the woman at ease. She wished she could tell her the whole story. Certainly no one had ever suspected *her* of being pregnant before. The idea made Maura's lips curve upward tentatively, trying the possibility on for size.

"Maura McNeill," announced the office nurse from the door to the inner sanctum. Grateful for the interruption, Maura set aside the dog-eared copy of *Mothers and Babies* and followed the sweet-faced nurse down the smoothly carpeted hall.

In a room no bigger than a minute, Maura suffered her finger to be pricked with a needle for the blood test. She had performed this test hundreds of times on other people, but she hated having it done to her. To distract herself, she looked around the room, pleased that everything looked clean and neat.

After taking her blood pressure, the office nurse briskly ushered Maura into a teak-paneled office and indicated a soft upholstered chair. "Dr. Copeland will be with you in a minute," she told Maura before turning on whisper-soft soles and closing the door gently behind her.

Maura's curious eyes swept his office, searching for clues to the man's personality. "Alexander Copeland, where are you?" she murmured to herself. There were no pictures of wife and kids, no trophies or medals or ornaments that would divulge anything about him. Just a wall full of somber-looking framed diplomas that attested to the medical degrees of Alexander Copeland, M.D., and a glass-fronted bookcase lined with dreary medical texts.

Dr. Copeland would be surprised, thought Maura, if he knew the real reason for her visit today. Maura had scheduled this appointment with Alexander Copeland, M.D., because he was the only obstetrician-gynecologist listed in the Shuffletown telephone directory. She required an obstetrician, all right, but not for any of the usual reasons.

As a certified nurse-midwife new to the area, Maura needed Dr. Copeland professionally, not personally. She had struck upon the novel idea of letting him perform a physical examination on her before she asked him to become her supervising physician. She wanted to find out firsthand if this Dr. Copeland was the kind of caring and involved doctor she would choose to provide emergency care for her patients once she set up her practice in midwifery.

The door opened so suddenly that it startled her. "Ms. McNeill?"

She looked up and up until her brown eyes ran across a strong chin punctuated by a deep cleft, and up some more to eyes of indeterminate color but fringed by the darkest, curliest lashes she'd ever seen on a man or a woman. His hair shaded from sable brown to black and waved crisply over his forehead, undaunted by the high humidity characteristic of this section of the United States.

Dr. Copeland shook Maura's hand briskly before walking around his desk and sitting down. *Why, he's younger than I expected,* she thought in surprise, realizing for the first time that she'd been expecting a grandfatherly type. He was in his mid- to late thirties, she'd guess. His attitude was entirely professional, and his eyes were kind. It was, she began to realize with dismay, her reaction to him that was the problem.

Alexander Copeland was, to put it bluntly, the most magnificent-looking man Maura had ever seen in all her twenty-eight years. The white coat he wore over his shirt and tie did absolutely nothing to moderate the effect of a marvelous broad-shouldered, lean-muscled physique. She swallowed, wondering how just looking at this man could bring on an attack of giddiness. Her stomach seemed to have migrated to her throat, which as a nurse-midwife she realized was a medical impossibility.

His eyes crinkled at the corners as he smiled. "So you're here today for a physical exam," he said encouragingly. These mundane words were doubtless the tried-and-true phrase he used with all new patients. She wondered if he was used to having a physical effect on his patients, or if he even knew he did.

"Yes," she said as coolly as she could, forgetting that her original purpose for this visit transcended a mere physical exam. Now she was feeling more physical by the minute.

"Anything special you want us to check?"

She must have answered his question, although she had no earthly idea what she'd said, because he stood up and told her, "My nurse will show you to my examining room, and I'll be with you in just a minute." He was still thoroughly professional, still entirely circumspect.

Now, Maura, she told herself sternly, *you're a medical professional. There's no reason for this man to create such havoc in you. Furthermore, you have no right to be thinking of shoulders in terms of broad or lips in terms of sensual.*

While Maura was thus dismissing the words "broad shoulders" and "sensual lips" from her mental space, the nurse appeared from somewhere and conducted Maura into another small room, where she instructed, "Take off all your clothes and wrap that sheet around you," before disappearing again.

Maura did as she was told, shivering into a mass of goose bumps in the blast from the air-conditioning vent. She wound herself in the sheet, slipped her shoes back on and then nervously slipped them off again, tiptoeing barefoot to the examining table. There was a stool there, and she stepped on it to boost herself onto the table.

She sat quietly for a moment before catching a glimpse of her distorted image in the shiny rectangular surface of the stainless-steel paper-towel holder over the sink. Her abundant auburn hair faded to an unattractive shade of orange under the bright fluorescent ceiling light, and her tawny complexion seemed pasty and washed out. Clutching the sheet to her chest for warmth, knees pressed tightly together, she lay back on the hard, paper-covered table and waited, conscious as never before of her own skin and how much of it wasn't covered by the skimpy sheet.

And here it came again, the stealthily encroaching memory of the way Dr. Copeland had looked as he sat across the desk from her. A bronzed face, which according to the laws of probability meant he spent a good deal of time outdoors, and smooth dark eyebrows that looked as though they could quirk upward with humor. She had noted an awkwardness about his nose that she hadn't quite absorbed. His nose was straight, but there was something odd about it, too. A slight lump about halfway down the length of his nose, that was it! That one minor flaw kept him from being too perfectly formed, which was probably a good thing. Lord knows, there was nothing wrong with the rest of him.

The minutes ticked by as she lay there, feeling increasingly defenseless in her nakedness. Her hipbones thrust rounded points upward beneath the sheet, which barely covered the curve of her thighs. Nervously she twitched the sheet downward, exposing the side of one shapely breast. She readjusted the fabric and forced herself to fold her hands modestly over her midriff. Strange, but she'd never thought of herself as having a body before. Well, a body, *yes*, for eating and sleeping. But she had learned to dismiss physical discomforts as unimportant, and lying on this table, she felt distinctly uncomfortable.

She tried counting the holes in the acoustical ceiling, but soon lost count. She didn't want to think about Dr. Copeland, but what else was there to think about? At least she could make an effort not to review his physical attributes. She wondered about his position regarding midwifery; there was a rivalry between the obstetrical and midwifery professions, each distrusting the other. Dr. Copeland was young enough to be open-minded, perhaps, but he was bound to be influenced by his traditional medical training. And then, without interrupting her flow of thought, she found herself thinking about the deep resonant timbre of his voice. It was low and melodious, the kind of voice you could listen to until you fell asleep beneath the caress of it.

The nurse came in. "Everything all right?" she asked brightly.

"Fine," said Maura to the ceiling, wondering if this could be counted as a lie. The nurse arranged assorted instruments on a tray and slipped out again, humming as she went.

Maura closed her eyes, but she couldn't keep Dr. Copeland's face out of her thoughts. It kept invading her consciousness, spreading itself across the inside of her eyelids like some wonderful new kind of wraparound visual effect. The vision transmuted itself into something closely approximating reality, a daydream and a half.

Soon, she thought dreamily, floating along with it, he would be standing above her, lifting aside the soft fabric of the sheet, his smooth fingers conducting their examination in a totally impersonal way. Her shoulders tensed forward protectively when she imagined his eyes sweeping her compliant body. To her amazement and utter chagrin, her nipples stiffened beneath the sheet at the very thought of his strong hands, alien and so male, touching her skin.

Aghast at this unexpected and purely physical response, she sat up abruptly and slid off the table, tearing the paper beneath her in her haste. She had been taught to dismiss physical discomforts—and physical pleasures as well. But now it seemed that banishing either was impossible.

All at once, irrationally and with a touch of sheer panic, she knew beyond a doubt that she couldn't do it; she couldn't allow Alexander Copeland to see her body awakening to his touch. She wasn't ready to be touched by a very virile and desirable man. Maybe she never would be.

Swiftly, reacting solely from her own blind instinct, she tossed aside the sheet and pulled on her plain white cotton underwear, then the bright print blouse borrowed from Kathleen, then her own ordinary tan cotton skirt. She didn't want to take the time to put on her panty hose, so she stuffed them in her handbag, not caring in the least whether they snagged or not.

Maura careered out of the examining room, almost knocking the sweet-faced nurse down in her hurry.

"I just remembered another appointment!" she

blurted at the nurse, to the other's utter amazement. And this, Maura knew, was definitely a lie.

And then she rushed through the waiting room, the startled faces of the pregnant patients all a blur, and out into the dank, oppressive humidity of early afternoon.

Maura's heart pounded as she fled across the street to the hospital parking lot and climbed into the decrepit old van that had carried her in temperamental fits and starts all the way across the continent. She couldn't help feeling that with her uncharacteristically crazy flight out of Dr. Copeland's office, she had blown her only chance to get a physician to supervise her practice in midwifery.

Oh, what was wrong with her? She'd thought she was adjusting to her new life, she'd thought everything was coasting along beautifully until she'd been confronted with Dr. Alexander Copeland. All he had done was speak a few ultraordinary sentences to her, nothing even slightly suggestive. And she had reacted like a frightened adolescent, not a grown woman—and a woman who was a nurse, at that. She rested her elbows on the sticky steering wheel and pressed her fingers to her temples, digging the heels of her hands into her eye sockets as though to rub out Dr. Copeland's handsome lingering image.

Well, she couldn't work with Alexander Copeland on a personal basis. That was perfectly clear. Her sexuality, she thought with a stab of despair, was as yet too new, too untried to be subjected to such a man.

It was several minutes before she composed herself enough to fit the key into the ignition and start the motor. Much as she needed a physician to supervise her practice in midwifery, much as she required dependable medical backup, she'd have to find somebody else, somebody safe, even if it meant going all the way to Charleston to find him.

Driving distractedly along the Shuffletown highway, she wondered how she'd ever be able to face Alexander Copeland again. Her inappropriate response to him forced her to see that she was going to have to relate to men in a new way in this, her new life, just as Kathleen had all too often cautioned her. At the moment Maura was feeling her sister's advice very strongly. She missed her comfortable old identity like a newly amputated limb. She was like the amputees she'd seen in the wards during her nurse's training: she felt as though a very important part of her had been cut off, and she could still feel the phantom ache of it at times.

When she first noticed the smell of burnt rubber, she was about a mile from the turnoff for the Teoway Island bridge. She sniffed the air, hoping that the acrid odor wasn't coming from her van. Then a dashboard light flashed on, and she pulled over to the side of the highway in alarm.

Maura was standing forlornly on the deserted road worrying about the wildly smoking engine and wishing she knew something about automobile mechanics when a small brown girl leaped out of the shrubbery. "Mama's going to have a baby!" blurted the child.

And then the girl started babbling, making very little sense at all to Maura. She was clearly in a panic, looking for someone, anyone to help.

Maura put her arm around the child's shoulders and knelt down beside her so that she would be at child's eye level. Her gentle touch seemed to have a calming effect. "Slow down," she said quietly and with an encouraging smile. "I can't understand what you're saying."

The chocolate-brown eyes blinked and a tear rolled down one plump cheek. The girl was still rattled, but no longer incoherent. "Please," implored the child, tugging frantically at Maura's hand. "Come quick. My mama's having a baby."

And so without stopping to ask any more questions, trying her best to cope with the world and whatever it demanded of her, Maura grabbed her midwife's bag off the cot in the back of the van and followed the child down the rutted dirt path at a run. On this one occasion, it seemed, her unreliable old van had broken down in just the right place at the right time to do somebody some good.

But then, she thought grimly, it was the only bright spot in a day when everything seemed to be going awry.

Chapter Two

The glare of the low-lying South Carolina sunset was muted in this shadowed room where filtered light touched the liquid dark eyes and high cheekbones of the black woman laboring on the bed.

Maura brushed a strand of her own auburn hair back behind her ear and summoned up all the feeling and intuition of her art. Gently she stroked the woman's damp brow, concentrating on focusing her own abundant energy so that the woman might draw strength from it.

"Push, Annie," she said, her voice low and vibrant with emotion. No matter how many babies she delivered, Maura never failed to feel the reverence for new life, the respect for the dignity of motherhood that she had experienced at her first birthing. The emotional and spiritual aspects of the art of midwifery were what made this calling so special to her.

Annie rolled her eyes and looked frightened. Maura felt a stab of doubt about the situation. But what could she expect from this woman? Annie had never laid eyes on Maura until a few short hours ago. It was Maura's responsibility to reassure her.

Maura knew that Annie was afraid of the sensations of labor; she needed to slow down. She slipped around the edge of the bed and eased herself down beside her. "Slow your breathing," she urged, placing Annie's hand on her own flat abdomen and demonstrating how to draw each breath slower and deeper than before.

Annie relaxed visibly, smiling as she became centered within herself and therefore less tense. She raised grateful eyes to Maura's. "Sure am glad you happened along," she said to Maura.

"I am, too," Maura told her warmly. She glanced at the small girl who hung over the back of a spraddle-legged straight chair in a corner, watching the proceedings with fascinated interest.

"You all right, Cindy?" Annie asked anxiously, craning her neck so she could see her daughter.

"Yes, Mama," said the child.

"Any time you want to leave, you go on," Annie told Cindy.

"I want to be with you, Mama," said Cindy.

Annie took a deep breath. "That's good. It makes me feel better having you near."

Annie's labor was well advanced, and there was no telephone. If Maura hadn't come along, Annie would have delivered her baby in fear and pain with only her own eight-year-old daughter in attendance.

The fact of this family's privation had been evident from the moment Maura saw the shack with its tarpaper roof and the porch leaning haphazardly to one side. "Such poverty!" she had muttered to herself. Her anger at such need, only a stone's throw away from the exclusive resort and residential community of Teoway Island, had taken second place, however, to her sense of purpose when she had beheld the frightened young woman on the sagging double bed in one of the cabin's two rooms.

"I sent Cindy up to the store to call Dr. Copeland around noon," Annie had told her shyly after Maura had quickly explained that she was a nurse-midwife and qualified to deliver Annie's baby. "Told him I couldn't get to the hospital and asked him to come here. Don't think he'll be here now." Annie's voice was meek and accepting.

There was no car in the weed-filled yard, no near neighbor that Maura could see. How had Dr. Copeland expected this woman to get to the hospital in the first place? By the ninth month of her pregnancy, he should have known Annie well enough to understand her isolated situation.

Doctors. They knew all about the latest technology. But what they didn't, wouldn't, understand was that childbirth couldn't be confined to science. Birthing required caring and involvement, something that most doctors seemed to know nothing about. Right now, while Annie was working hard to deliver this baby, Alexander Copeland was probably relaxing in the cocktail lounge at the Teoway Island Inn, bragging about his golf game.

Oh, Maura hadn't forgotten her own lightning re-

sponse to his innate sensuality. But she was glad to find
out exactly what kind of lackadaisical doctor he really
was. In her own mind, this new perception of him justi-
fied her precipitous leave-taking this afternoon.

Now Maura reached for the lip balm in her bag and
deftly applied it to Annie's parched lips. "Would you
like a lozenge?" she asked Annie after the next contraction.

"A what?"

"A hard candy. So your mouth won't feel dry."

"Oh, yes."

Maura placed the lozenge on Annie's tongue, and
Annie's eyes drifted closed in relief.

Earlier Maura had drawn the ragged shades over the
windows to block out the scorching rays of the sun, but
the sun penetrated the shades anyway through tiny
holes torn in the plastic. Perspiration beaded Maura's
forehead and soaked the back of her blouse and the
smock she wore to protect her clothes. She raised one
of the shades a few inches to admit some fresh air, although there was no breeze in this heavily wooded
place.

The moisture-drenched air in the cabin was hot, too
hot, and she sponged Annie's face with a damp rag.
"Get me some more water from the pump, will you,
honey?" she asked Cindy.

Cindy said, "Yes'm," and scampered away to the
hand-operated pump in the yard from which water reluctantly trickled forth. There wasn't any electricity.
The water had to be boiled over an old wood-burning
stove in a corner of the other room.

Maura stood, lacing her fingers behind her back and raising her arms in a yoga exercise to relieve the tension in her shoulder muscles. Labor coaching was always hard work.

She sat down again and wrung the cloth out with fresh cool water from the bucket. She watched Annie carefully, timing Annie's contractions. Cindy brought a palm-leaf fan and waved it over the bed to stir up the heavy, hot air.

"Oh!" Annie gasped suddenly, her spine suddenly going rigid with a new contraction. "The baby's coming!"

Maura jumped to her feet and bent over the bed, checking. It was true. One good strong contraction had made the birth imminent. "Good, Annie," she encouraged. "A good, strong push." And then, crooning, "Come on, baby. That's right."

The baby's head was in view now. Its head and—oh, no!—a tiny arm. This was a compound presentation, a complication. Maura caught her breath in consternation, observing the small head carefully. Everything looked fine, except for that little arm. Its presence meant that the baby's head would have to be rotated and the arm drawn gently forward so that the shoulders could be born.

What a time for a motorcycle to skid into the yard, shooting out sand and gravel in a semicircle like a scene from the television show *CHIPs*! Maura spared the motorcycle and its rider only a quick glance through the gap between shade and windowsill. She didn't have time to speculate about who it was and what he might be doing in this godforsaken place. She was summoning all her knowledge of midwifery, all the skill and learning within her, to safely deliver Annie's baby.

As usual at birthings, Maura was the only one with the skill and expertise to provide a healthy delivery for both mother and child. Everything, absolutely everything, depended on her.

XAN COPELAND SLID from the seat of his bright blue Honda and propped it on its kickstand. It didn't want to stay propped because the earth here was too soft, so he looked around for a rock and nudged it beneath the stand with his toe so the bike wouldn't fall over. Then he turned and sized up the wooden shack.

Typical, and just what he had expected. Mrs. Annie Bodkin had seen him for prenatal care, all right. Exactly twice. Then she had dropped out of sight and he hadn't heard a word from her until today when a child had telephoned and summoned him to her mother's bedside, where, the child said in a quavery voice, she was "gonna have a baby, and pretty quick, too."

He should have ignored the call for help; Quinby Hospital had a rule that only mothers who had been seen regularly for prenatal care were to be admitted. With Annie Bodkin, there was no possibility of hospital admittance, but he'd wanted to do something to help her. He recalled her tight, scared face on the two occasions when she'd shown up for her checkups.

Well, he had tried, but he hadn't been able to get to Annie right away because just as he was about to leave his office, the hospital had called with the news that one of his regular patients was about to deliver twins and it looked like a cesarean, and the ensuing hubbub had made him forget all about Mrs. Annie Bodkin until he was showering afterward. He had dressed quickly, hopped on his bike and raced over here, taking several wrong turns before he found the isolated cabin.

He ignored the stairs, which looked so rotten that he doubted they would hold his weight, and bounded directly onto the porch. When nobody answered his urgent knock, he pulled at the flimsy screen door until it swung open.

He glanced swiftly around the room, a combination cooking and eating and living room. A door led to another room and he strode to it. He wasn't at all prepared for what he saw.

Annie lay on the bed giving birth. That registered immediately. But who was assisting her? This redhead whose hair sparkled with the fire of rubies in the streamers of light beaming through the holes in the ragged window shades?

His first impulse was to rush to the bed and impose his presence on the two women, but something made him stop dead in his tracks. It was the redhead with the long bare arms. Her arms were what he noticed about her most, after her red hair. At the moment those arms were employed in an activity about which he thought he knew everything, but he'd never before seen anyone delivering a baby with such grace, such rhythm.

She made a kind of ballet out of it, raised it from the ordinary to the sublime, if such a thing were possible. She bent gracefully over the bed and the woman, coordinating the motion of her shoulders and arms and hands and hips to Annie's needs. Watching her, he was transfixed at the subtle and intuitive movements, at the spirituality of the process.

"Annie, everything is wonderful, everything is fine," she said, and her voice was low and husky and gentle, almost hypnotic in its effect. It was then that he realized with a start that this was Maura McNeill, the woman he'd seen in his office earlier, the one who had caused a great deal of consternation among his office staff by bolting and running from the examining room.

Now, through eyes narrowed in speculation, he permitted himself to look at her, to *really* look at her as a man looks at a woman. It was a luxury he never allowed himself when seeing patients.

She wasn't a glamour girl, that was evident. She was strong, a strong woman, and she looked sensible. And sensitive, too, he could tell by the curves of her mouth. He hated weak-mouthed women, but she wasn't one of them. He liked to see a full bottom lip, which she had, with a generously bowed top lip. Her teeth were square and white and even.

Oh, but there was something wrong! As his eyes grew more accustomed to the dim light in the room, his breath tightened apprehensively in his throat as he realized that the birth was a compound presentation! The infant's hand was presenting alongside its ear. He was ready to run back to his bike to get his bag when Maura glanced quickly back over her shoulder toward the gloomy corner where he stood and smiled coolly.

The smile staggered him. Such glowing beauty in these miserable surroundings seemed out of place enough, but it was what was behind the smile that almost knocked him over. A competence, a reassurance. *She* was reassuring *him*?

But wait—she was grasping the infant's hand and rotating its head, exactly as he would have done, and far more gently, too. She was no blundering amateur at this. She knew what she was doing. That thought set him back almost as much as the smile. He backed off, leaned against the wall and watched. He wanted to see what she'd do next.

Maura carefully extracted the baby's arm, and in a rush the shoulders followed. Almost immediately the baby slid free. Her voice rang with exuberance and triumph as the baby settled into her broad hands. "A boy, Annie!" she proclaimed with great joy and feeling. "A wonderful, beautiful boy!"

Annie, beaming, reached for the baby, which immediately rent the humid air with a lusty cry. Maura, with a beatific radiance on her face, gently arranged the tiny infant in Annie's arms.

Cindy crept close to the bed, her round eyes filled with awe and wonder, and wordlessly Maura drew her to Annie so that Cindy could lay her small brown cheek against her mother's. It was a tableau so touching and so moving that Xan Copeland felt the sting of tears in his eyes.

Damn! This was ridiculous. How many births had he witnessed by this time? Hundreds? Thousands? And yet not one had been accompanied by the sensitivity or the love he had witnessed here, in this ugly shack.

He blinked rapidly, once, twice. When his eyes cleared, he saw that Maura, knowing exactly what she was about, was taking care of business. Her hair, which had been drawn back in a loose clip, fell free now. It crowned her, made her seem almost madonna-like, her hair a mantle of loveliness draping over her square shoulders, softening the angular planes of her face. Unmindful of its beauty, she flipped her head so that her hair arced through the air, threading the fading rays of the sun with brilliance.

He continued to watch silently. She knew he was watching, of course, but she had so many things to think about that she didn't have time to worry about him. She certainly hadn't recognized him as Alexander Copeland. She was just grateful he hadn't passed out when he'd bumbled unexpectedly onto a woman giving birth. Some men would have.

Annie murmured to her new son, a good sign of bonding. The baby in its mother's arms seemed still a part of its mother until it stirred, its mouth seeking sustenance. Maura guided the tiny mouth toward the maternal breast. As mouth opened to receive nipple, the mother sighed peacefully. The tranquillity of mother and child reached out to embrace Maura, making her feel marvelously in tune with the world and everything in it.

When she was certain she could be spared, Maura straightened, massaged the aching hollow of her back for a moment and shot the man leaning against the wall a tentative smile. It was then that she recognized with a sudden spine-tingling shock who he was.

Dr. Copeland! Oh, no! Maura's knees actually gave way for a moment as her eyes widened in astonishment. She held on to the flaking iron bedstead for support as she felt her cheeks flame red in embarrassment.

But then, when the first flash of recognition had passed, she was stunned to see a look of grudging admiration on his face. She tried to get a handle on her runaway thoughts, to see this from his point of view. She was sure that he didn't think she belonged here, but she had handled a difficult delivery well, partly out of instinct, partly out of her finesse as a midwife. She had reason to be proud of herself, but it was clear that she'd better explain.

She drew a deep breath and let go of the bedstead, not sure whether her knees were operative or not. They held her up, however, which was more than she'd expected. She motioned toward the door with her head, dreading the confrontation with him, and he followed her as she walked very carefully, putting one foot deliberately in front of the other, into the other room.

"Dr. Copeland, about what happened," she began uneasily, turning to face him.

Interrupting, he said, "Call me Xan. And don't apologize. You were good in there."

As luck would have it, he was going to be nice about it. It wasn't what she had expected from him at all. She managed to smile in relief as she brushed a wisp of hair off her forehead. "Thanks," she said. A pang of guilt speared through her as she thought about running out of his office earlier. Tired as she was, she was still aware of his all-too-virile attraction. To distract herself from his sex appeal, she said, "Do you mind if I fix tea?"

"Not at all," he said. "May I help?" He was letting her remain in charge; this too surprised her.

"You could find a teapot," she said as she set out the cups. She wasn't used to doctors doing her bidding.

He rummaged in an old cracked cupboard until his fingers closed around the spout of a pot. He handed the pot to Maura, who poured boiling water over a handful of dried herbs and set the teapot aside to steep.

As she worked efficiently and with practiced economy of movement, she observed Xan Copeland surreptitiously out of the corner of her eyes, thinking that it was no wonder she hadn't recognized him when he first came in. Now he wore an ordinary knit shirt, green with a blue alligator on it, not the shirt and tie and white coat he'd worn in the office today. He hadn't buttoned any of the buttons on the alligator shirt, and sprigs of tightly curled black hair sprang through the placket.

After he found the teapot, he stood watching with his arms folded over his chest, muscular arms, and his shoulders were so broad that she thought he should probably have bought the next size larger shirt. Below that his blue jeans looked well-worn. And he should have bought a larger size in those, too.

"What are you doing here?" he asked flatly.

Uh-oh, here it comes, she thought with dread. She braced herself for condemnation—or at the very least, criticism. "Nothing I'm not qualified to do," she said firmly.

"I could see that," he assured her. He smiled reluctantly, and when she smiled back in surprise he realized in equal surprise that they were sharing this experience. He felt a specific feeling, almost as though a specialized nerve was shooting the message to his brain and other vital places that this woman was one he wanted to know better—much better.

It was twilight now, birds chirping in the surrounding woods as they flew home to roost. Heat radiated from the wood-burning stove, warming the room to a temperature fit for neither man nor beast. "Come out on the porch," he said persuasively, suddenly wanting her to be comfortable. "It'll be cooler there."

Concern for her patient overrode any consideration of her own comfort, and Maura sent an anxious look toward the doorway. "Annie needs to be checked every ten minutes or so."

"I know that," he said warmly. "Come on, you look exhausted." He guided her toward the door with a sure hand on her upper arm, a touch that, despite her fatigue, reawakened her senses.

Xan liked the way she walked as she preceded him

out the door. Her walk was a glide, very smooth, with nothing of the coquette about it. He had never seen such magnificent hair, a complex of reds reflecting light from every strand so that its swinging weight seemed electrified in its radiance.

Two very ordinary slat-backed rocking chairs occupied the porch. "Oh, my, does it ever feel wonderful to sit down!" she exclaimed fervently as she sank down on one rocking chair and he sat on the other.

"How long have you been delivering babies?" he asked.

"Several years," she said, trying to get in the habit of looking at a man in a different way from the way she always had before. Here in the twilight the color of his eyes was no longer in question. They were a deep and mossy shade of green, and at the moment they were scrutinizing her, taking everything in. His overt examination made her feel even more self-conscious.

"I guess I could take this smock off now," she said, grappling with the button and loop in back. She had thrown it on hurriedly over the print blouse on loan from Kathleen and her own tan skirt.

Without saying a word, he stood up and, standing behind her chair, reached for the button. The move startled her, and as their fingers brushed she yanked her own hands away.

"Please don't jump like that," he heard himself saying as he pushed the button through its loop. "I only wanted to touch your hair, your splendorous hair. Unbuttoning this smock for you provides the perfect excuse." Quickly and unexpectedly he ran exploratory fingers up the back of her neck and fanned them through the strands of auburn divided on either side of the smock fastening. Then, sensing her stunned shrinking away from him, he raked his fingers downward and let the heavy tresses fall back into place.

The blush rose upward from somewhere in her stomach region, heating the skin of her chest, staining her neck. Still, she didn't say anything, because she was too shocked at this touching of her person to object. But no one in the past had ever reached through her invisible cloak of dignity to touch her, and most particularly not in such an overtly sexual manner!

To hide her confusion, she bent slightly forward to shrug out of the smock as Xan returned to his chair, and the motion inadvertently tugged the neckline of her blouse out of place to reveal the soft, smooth swell of the top of her breasts swinging unfettered beneath the thin fabric.

It was the glimpse of that womanly part of her that did him in. Xan knew in that moment that he wanted to ensure that there would be other meetings in other places more conducive to—well, what? He had been about to think the word love, but love wasn't something he ever thought about. Women, yes. Lust, yes. After all, he was thirty-seven years old, very eligible, and no one these days expected an eligible bachelor to be a saint. But love?

Xan made it a policy never to date his patients. He wasn't sure, since she had run away before he'd actually examined her, if she could be considered a patient. "Why did you run away this afternoon?" he asked.

She could never tell him that. Not in a million years. "Because I changed my mind," she retorted, willing the blush to fade.

"Something wrong with my office staff? Something about me that offended you?" His voice was gruff, and his eyes burned into her as though they could see the very corners of her soul.

"I—had another appointment," she said weakly.

"Nonsense. There must have been more to it than that. Since you're a midwife yourself, I can hardly imagine that you would be squeamish about the physical part of the examination."

"No, of course not," she said. "I had another appointment. Can't we let it go at that?"

He paused to think about it. "For the time being, I suppose we can," he said, relenting out of kindness. She appeared shaken. He looked at her, reappraising her. He'd thought she was sensible, and he still thought so. But there was a vulnerability in her gentle, soft eyes. He liked the way her magnificently high and elegantly constructed cheekbones curved precisely into long planes ending in a strong jaw and squared-off chin. Despite the vulnerability, it was altogether a face of strong character. She must have a good reason for being evasive.

"Well, then," Xan said lightly, "let's talk about something else."

"Must we talk?" she said, her voice trembling

even though she fought to control it. "I'm exhausted."

"You're all wrought up from the emotion in there," he said, gesturing toward the door of the cabin. "Talking will help coast you down from that high you're on."

"So you know about that," she said wonderingly.

"Of course. I feel it myself. Often after a difficult delivery I go home so revved up I can't sleep. It's then that I wish there was someone to talk to so I could wind down."

"You have no one?"

"I live alone," he said, and the conversation paused for several beats while she took in the significance of this statement. Then he said more quietly, his voice low, "How did you happen to be here when Annie needed you?"

"The question I have is, how did you happen not to be here when she needed you? She's your patient." Maura met his eyes with a boldness that he would not have expected from her. Nor would she have expected it from herself a few short months ago. But now such audacity was emerging as part of her character.

She had put him on the defensive, but he respected her for it. In fact he would have had the same question if their places had been reversed.

Quickly he told her how Cindy had called just before he'd had to report to the hospital to deliver twins, and how he hadn't seen Annie Bodkin since the first two times she'd visited him for prenatal care. "Really," he told her, "I'm glad you were here." His eyes shone with sincerity, and Maura was astonished. She had thought he would be jealous of her competence or, at the very least, overly defensive.

"I wouldn't have been here either if my van hadn't broken down," said Maura.

Xan recalled that when he'd been looking for the Bodkins' house, he'd been curious about the scabrous white van with its splayed and worn tires. He'd thought it looked out of place on the lonely stretch of road. "Is your van the one next to the Shuffletown highway with Pringle's Florists—We Deliver on its side?"

She laughed, easing up a bit. "That's right. I've only had the van for a couple of months. I'm going to paint over the Pringle's Florists part, but I thought I'd leave on the We Deliver."

"You're so right—it is appropriate," he said, and they laughed together. It made him happy to see her relaxing, letting go.

When they had stopped laughing and the silence grew up around them, he said carefully, "Sounds as though you're stuck here with no way to get home."

"I guess so. Just one thing—do we consider Annie your patient or mine?" There was a hint of trepidation in her voice.

"Ours," he said immediately. "Hey, don't you understand I'm not going to make trouble for you? You did a fine job. Why don't you continue to care for Annie and her baby if it will make you happy?"

Maura suddenly saw clearly that she was going to have to revise her opinion of Dr. Copeland's lackadaisical attitude. It was plain to see that Xan Copeland was a warm, caring physician, as dedicated as they come. Never mind the machismo, never mind the overwhelming sensuality. Underneath the perfect packaging, he was exactly the kind of doctor she would choose to supervise her practice. Ah, but if only he would! How could she work around to that question? And even if he would, did she want him to? It would mean close contact with him from time to time, and she wasn't sure she could handle that.

But first things first. "If I'm going to continue to care for Annie and the baby, I won't be able to leave for a while," she said. "I'll need to watch them for a couple of hours to make sure everything is okay with both of them. In fact," she said, glancing at her no-nonsense nurse's watch, "I'd better look in on them now and take Annie a cup of herbal tea. Would you care for tea?"

Xan would have rather had a cold beer, but looking straight into Maura's level brown eyes—and he hadn't seen too many brown-eyed redheads in his time—he surprised himself by saying, "Sure."

After she took Annie the tea, Maura poured a cup of tea for herself and one for Xan. "I had to sweeten the tea with sugar because that's all there is," she apologized as she handed him the cup. "I would have preferred honey."

"Oh? Are you one of these health-food freaks, into alfalfa sprouts and things like that?"

"Do you have something against alfalfa sprouts?" she asked.

"Only that I can't eat them without getting them caught between my teeth," he said.

She stared at him, deflected from her defensive stance by his humor. Then she started to laugh. "Well, try the tea. It's a special herbal blend and very relaxing."

"If I relax any more, I may fall out of this rocking chair," he said.

"In California, we'd call you laid-back," said Maura before realizing that she'd revealed too much.

"In South Carolina, it's called lazy," Xan shot back. "Anyway, is that where you're from? California?"

"Yes," she said in a tone that precluded any further inquiry about her past. She stood up so abruptly that the rocking chair tipped forward and smacked her against the back of her knees. In obvious agitation, she walked to the end of the porch and stared out into the dark woods. She hadn't meant to mention California. It had just slipped out.

Xan sipped the tea slowly. So she was from California, and she didn't want to talk about it, he thought. Interesting.

"I've been thinking," he said carefully. "I can check your van for you, see what's wrong. Maybe I can get it running again."

She turned toward him quickly, relieved at the change of subject almost as much as at his suggestion that he investigate the van's mechanical problem. "Would you look at it? I—I don't understand much about automobiles, and I'd be so grateful."

"Be glad to." He stood and set the cup of tea on a window ledge. Tension hung in the air between them; it had started when she had mentioned California and then had immediately become so skittish.

"Here, you'll need my keys," she said, fishing them out of her skirt pocket. She handed him her key ring.

"I'll check your van out and see what I can do for you," he said before wheeling and stepping off the porch without using the stairs.

In a moment, his Honda sputtered to life. Xan switched on the headlight, throwing a strong bright beam against the trees at the edge of the clearing. Then with a jaunty wave he was gone, a rooster tail of dust spurting out behind him.

Good, Maura thought to herself. She'd worried about the van and wondered how she was going to get it repaired. She certainly hadn't relished the idea of walking to the nearby crossroads store where Cindy had said there was a telephone. After her frantic trip across the continental United States in the van, she was thoroughly aware of her vulnerability as a lone woman on the highway. It would be totally dark before she was ready to leave here, and even if she did walk to the phone at the crossroads, she wouldn't have any idea which garage to call for help.

Maura sat back down in her rocking chair and wearily rested her head against the high back. Why had she said anything about California? That part of her life was over, done with, finis. She'd hopped in the van and set out blindly for the farthest sanctuary she knew, and she'd ended up here in South Carolina with Kathleen and Don.

Speaking of the van, she'd be lost without it. She hoped Xan could muster enough mechanical expertise to find and repair whatever was wrong with the motor.

ACCELERATING HIS HONDA down the overgrown path toward the highway, Xan also wondered what was wrong with Maura's van. Then a smile tugged at the corners of his mouth. It didn't matter what was wrong. He was going to make absolutely sure that she didn't leave this place in it.

In fact Maura would have been amazed to know that Xan had already decided that the only satisfactory mode of transportation for her tonight was his motorcycle, where she would ride behind him, her ample breasts pressed to his back, her long, tanned arms wrapped securely around his waist.

Chapter Three

While Xan was gone, Maura washed herself, dipping her hands over and over into the bucket of cool water from the pump. She splashed the water slowly over her face, her arms, her breasts, considering how it felt. She was used to washing her patients, but for herself this task had always been accomplished in the shortest possible time with absolutely no consideration of it as an exercise in creature comfort.

The water trickled in cool rivulets down the sides of her face, gathered in the hollows above her shoulder blades, ran slickly between her breasts, hung in heavy droplets from the pink tips of her nipples. The crude towel with which she patted herself dry was stiff until the water softened it. But noticing the textures that touched her body was new to her, and it felt good to cool off, although cooling off didn't do anything to dispel her weariness.

She did her best to keep Annie and the baby comfortable, and she taught Cindy a new variation of cat's cradle in order to pass the time. It seemed like forever before Xan returned. As soon as she heard the Honda thundering down the dirt road toward Annie's shack, Maura stopped folding clean cloths for the baby and hurried to the front door.

"I've had a friend tow your van to his garage," Xan told Maura when she stepped anxiously out on the porch, closing the screen door quietly behind her. "I don't have any idea what's wrong with it." This statement was accompanied by a shrug of his broad shoulders. His face, upturned toward her, picked up a glow from the light of the kerosene lamp Maura had lit inside.

"Well, then," she said, her expression decidedly woebegone, "I suppose the next problem is getting home."

"Where do you live?"

"I'm staying on Teoway Island."

For a moment satisfaction flickered in his eyes. This was better than he'd hoped. "My villa is on the island," he told her. "I'll be glad to give you a lift. That is, if you don't mind riding on the back of my motorcycle."

At this point, it felt good to let someone else take over. "I don't mind," she said.

"How's Annie?" he asked quickly, and not offhandedly, but as though it really mattered. By this time he had stepped up and joined her on the creaky front porch, placing himself only an arm's length away. Other than their voices, the only sound was that of crickets chirping in the bushes.

"Annie's doing beautifully, and so is the baby. I could leave now, I suppose."

As Xan grasped her possessively by the shoulders and turned her toward the house, his strength surged through her. And this time, because his touch didn't seem particularly sexual, she didn't think anything untoward about it.

"Why don't you get your things and say good-bye to everyone, and I'll take you home?" he suggested. "You look like you've had one very hard day."

She nodded dumbly, too tired to do anything else. As she stepped inside the cabin, she caught a glimpse of herself in a cracked mirror hanging beside the door. She looked worn to a frazzle. Her back ached, her shoulders felt bunched into knots, and at the moment she longed for nothing so much as a decent meal followed by a leisurely bath in the sunken tub at Kathleen's beautiful, well-appointed and expensive house overlooking the Teoway marshes.

Annie and Cindy and the baby were quickly settled for the night, and after a whispered good-bye to Annie and a promise to check on her again soon, Maura rejoined Xan on the front porch.

The air had cooled, thank goodness, now that darkness had dropped over the countryside. It was a clear night, the air moist but not muggy, and the stars overhead shone with a clarity unmasked by clouds. There was a moon, too, a great golden globe hanging so close that Maura felt all she had to do was reach up and touch it.

Xan slid a proprietary arm around her shoulders and divested her of her leather medical bag containing her midwife's kit. He handed her carefully down the steps as though he thought she or the stairs might break. At this point, Maura thought from inside her fog of fatigue, if anything broke, it would be her and not the flimsy stairs.

"Have you ever ridden on a motorcycle before?" he asked her with a grin. He was packing her bag into one of his commodious saddlebags and looking sideways up at her; the moonlight gilded his face and reflected twin moons from the dark pupils of his eyes.

She stared at him, caught up in the magic of the moons in his eyes. Then she smiled, thinking that if he knew anything at all about her previous life, he'd find this a ridiculous question. "No, never," she said, wishing she could tell him how funny this situation was to her.

"Here. Put on this helmet." He held it toward her. It was gold, with sparkly flecks in it. They shimmered in the moonlight.

Hesitantly she pulled the helmet over her head and tried to fasten the chin strap.

"That's not the way to do it," he chided, bending forward to snap it properly as he would a child's. She was tall, over five foot seven, and he still had to bend over. She wondered how tall he was. Six one? Six two?

He knit his brows, fascinated by the effect of Maura's wearing a motorcycle helmet. She looked fantastic, even with smudges of fatigue beneath her eyes. A shock of auburn hair fell over her forehead and the rest hung from beneath the helmet in a soft and beguiling fringe.

"Now hop on," he told her as he held the bike.

"You mean just—"

"Sure." He smiled encouragingly. It occurred to her that when they were riding, she'd have nothing to hold on to except him. This whole scene seemed as though it belonged to someone else's life, not hers. But she gamely hitched her skirt up above her knees and swung a leg over the bike.

He got on, too, and before she could change her mind, they were wheeling around the clearing, the roar of the engine rending the night. Her hair whipped out behind her, free as air. The wind danced on her face, and she felt as though she were flying. She surprised herself by laughing out loud, when just a few minutes ago she had felt so drained of energy that she never would have thought she'd be laughing.

"Do you like this?" Xan shouted over his shoulder. She could barely hear him with the noise of the wind rushing past.

"Yes!" she shouted back.

"That's why I keep a motorcycle as well as a car. Riding is one way for me to get rid of tension." His hair ruffled backward, caressing the side of her face as she inclined her head forward to hear his words.

She clutched Xan's midriff more tightly. Underneath his knit shirt he was spare and lean, just as he looked, with no roll of flab at his waist, only firm muscle.

Maura relaxed a bit when they pulled out on the deserted highway, and he relaxed, too. As his muscles untensed, he leaned backward slightly into her. The

sensation of his vibrating back pressed to her soft
breasts and flat belly was titillating, to say the least. It
was a wholly sensual feeling, suffusing her entire
body, sending warm ripples to the center of her, but
surprisingly, these sensations weren't unwelcome.
She swallowed at this new knowledge of herself and
looked over his shoulder, watching the white divider
lines on the road slide past.

The distance to Teoway Island was not as far in
miles as it was in cultural lag. Annie's cabin and
others like it were located along a lonely highway on
the mainland in a community aptly called Shuffletown
about twenty miles from the large and elegant city of
Charleston. Unincorporated, forgotten and ignored by
its well-to-do neighbors, Shuffletown housed the
mostly black population that had once worked the rich
South Carolina plantation land as slaves.

Staying on after the Civil War, they had become
tenant farmers, working the land for others. Some
made a living fishing the abundant waters off the
coast. Lately, many had found employment in the resort and residential developments on Teoway Island.
Others left for better-paying jobs in the cities, never to
return.

For those who remained in Shuffletown, life could
be good if they didn't expect too much in the way of
worldly goods. They were not wealthy by most people's standards, but there was one commodity that
they produced with abundance. Children.

Maura loved the children. Children with wide
gleaming smiles. Little girls with hair braided in corn-

rows, coffee-colored scalp shining between the rows. Small boys with tight black curls, chasing one another in play, their brown legs pumping as they ran. These children were not well-dressed, as their counterparts on Teoway Island were. They wore cotton shorts and simple shirts, some of them homemade. Or they wore T-shirts and jeans bought at rummage sales. Now, in the summer, they went barefoot.

Maura had first asked Kathleen about the Shuffletown community one day as they sat sunning themselves on exclusive Teoway Island's wide beach.

"No one on Teoway Island seems to know anything about Shuffletown," said Kathleen, dismissing her question with a shrug.

"Everyone who lives here has to cross the Teoway Island bridge to pass through Shuffletown on his way to Charleston," reasoned Maura.

"I don't think anyone from Teoway *wants* to know anything about Shuffletown," Kathleen had said pointedly.

And then Maura had dropped a bombshell. "I'm going to set up my practice in midwifery in Shuffletown," she declared. "I'm going to provide home births for the people who want them."

Her sister had stared in openmouthed shock. "Shuffletown is not the kind of place you'd want to practice as a midwife," Kathleen had demurred. "The people..." She had let her sentence taper off when she'd seen the determined look on Maura's face.

"They're the kind of people I want to serve, the kind of people I worked with in California," Maura replied quietly. "They need me, Kath." Maura didn't know if Kathleen was being purposely obtuse or if she really, after all their sisterly talks, didn't understand why Maura had left California and everything there for a new life, a life she fervently hoped would be more purposeful than the old one.

"I don't know about people here going for home births," Kathleen had argued. "This section of the country isn't as modern as California, you know. People here are much more traditionally oriented."

"Women everywhere are opting for home births when it's possible. I'll help them to understand what a home birth is about, just the way I did with the people in the city ghetto. Believe me, I know from experience that there will be lots of pregnant women who prefer to birth their babies at home. Besides, I already know that there's no practicing midwife in this area."

"Don't people equate midwives with the old country women who used to deliver babies?" asked Kathleen with a worried frown. "I'm sure they don't understand that midwifery is a nursing specialty, and that one of its requirements is advanced study in addition to a degree in nursing."

"People usually look at me askance when I ask about midwives," conceded Maura. "But I've never actually told anyone here that I'm a midwife."

Kathleen stared. "Why not? It's hardly something to be ashamed of."

"You know I'm proud of my calling," Maura said. "It's just that it wouldn't be in my best interest to be too open about it yet."

"Whatever you say," Kathleen had sighed, knowing better than to brook Maura's stubborn determination, and so Maura had persistently made discreet inquiries in Shuffletown at places where people gathered—small stores and gas stations and hole-in-the-wall cafés. She'd deliberately avoided Quinby Hospital, which served this area. She wasn't ready to let anyone in the health-care professions know she was here. She could hardly expect the local doctors to welcome her with open arms, after all. She was a threat to their business, to their very livelihood.

Today, she thought wryly, by delivering Annie Bodkin's baby, she had revealed her secret. Unexpectedly, and before she had all her ducks in a row, before she had figured out how to manage financially—and aside from the problem of finding a sponsoring obstetrician, money was her biggest worry. Well, that was the way of it. Birthing babies didn't run by time schedules, or financial schedules, either.

Ahead of Xan's motorcycle, the trees arching over the road to Teoway Island streaked the road with shadows. The roar of the Honda had faded to a hum now that Maura was used to it, and the vibration somehow soothed her tired body. She fought the entirely human urge to rest her cheek against Xan's broad back.

"When was the last time you ate?" he shouted. His words were all but whipped away by the wind.

"Before Annie's baby was born," she said, her lips close to Xan's ear, so close she could smell the warm natural fragrance of his skin.

Without warning, he swerved the motorcycle into the shell-rock parking lot of a small roadside diner and cut the engine. "Will you join me for dinner?" he said, sliding partway off the motorcycle and switching on his considerable charm as he half turned to look at her in the flash of the blinking red neon lights.

"Here?" She looked at the diner, which shook on its foundations with twangy country music from a blaring jukebox.

"I know it's not as fancy as the Teoway Island Inn," he said persuasively, "but they fry a mean chicken. We'll have to ask them if they have alfalfa sprouts."

She smiled back. He was nice; he really was. She honestly didn't think he realized what a sensory effect he was having on her.

"Even if they don't have sprouts, they could grow them in a week or so. I'd be glad to describe the process." She lifted the helmet off her head and let her hair spill out over her shoulders.

"I'd rather you describe how you came by such gorgeous hair," he said, lifting a strand of it and letting it flow through his fingers like liquid copper.

"That's easy," she said lightly. "I was born with it." She flipped her head so that her hair was out of his reach and strode toward the door, not wanting the conversation to take a more serious turn.

"Birthing, borning," he said, following her. "With you everything seems to revolve around such things." He sounded serious, but at the same time not.

She glanced back over her shoulder with a smile.

"The whole world revolves around such things. Can you think of anything that's more important?" And she was utterly serious.

He shook his head thoughtfully as he held the door open for her. Her retort had given him pause. "I guess not," he conceded.

Inside, people bunched around a long counter watching a baseball game on television. Raucous laughter echoed off the dingy beige walls, but Xan steered Maura to the end booth, where, blessedly, the music and laughter were muted.

"I apologize for the place," he said. "We could have gone to the inn, but I thought you might prefer not to have to go home and dress first. I know you're tired." He was looking at her with empathy.

"You're right," she said gratefully. "Have you ever noticed how birthing babies fills you up in one way but depletes you in another?"

"Of course," he said, a surprised yet meditative expression flitting across his face. It was the way he often felt himself, but he hadn't before known anyone to whom he could communicate such feelings. As nothing else could have, her voicing of his own thoughts gave a more meaningful significance to his attraction to her.

After they had ordered, Xan studied her with absorbed concentration over the chipped Formica table. "So," he said, "tell me all about being a midwife."

"It seems to me that you saw all there was to see about it back at Annie's house," she said, smiling at him.

He laughed. "You're right. What I can't figure out is why you're here in Shuffletown."

"I'm visiting my sister and her husband, Don and Kathleen O'Malley," she told him. "Don's the resident pro at the Teoway Island tennis club. Do you know them?"

"I run into them at parties now and then. I play tennis with Don occasionally, when he's looking for someone he can beat without too much trouble," said Xan. Now that she had told him who her sister was, he could see her resemblance to Kathleen, although they were two different types, that was for sure. Kathleen was the glossy one, ajangle with jewelry and the latest fashions; he'd always thought she was pretty. But Maura was thoughtful and tranquil and intelligent and above all completely natural, and he thought she was beautiful.

"Do you play tennis?" he asked hopefully.

She shook her head, her hair rippling across her shoulders in a fascinating show. "Seldom," she said. She wasn't going to let him maneuver her into a dating situation, no matter how casual. There wasn't space for that in her life right now; she needed time to figure out just where men fit into it—if they fit at all.

"Well, we'll have to remedy that," he said, crinkling his eyes coaxingly. "How about a doubles match with Kathleen and Don some evening?"

"Sorry, but tennis isn't on my list of priorities."

Xan was taken aback by her refusal. He wasn't used to being turned down by women. "Well," he said, realizing he was up against something new, "what are your priorities?" His eyes, richly green now, were suddenly intent.

This intensity caught her attention, and his receptiveness warmed her and made her want to confide in him. Birthing Annie's baby had opened a floodgate of emotion for her. It had been too long since she had felt the joy of a tiny body settling into her hands, since she'd thrilled to that welcome first cry of a newborn. Xan was a doctor, yes, but he had also proved himself to be extraordinarily caring and interested. She thought he'd understand.

She drew a deep breath. "My first priority at the moment is setting up my own practice in midwifery, right here in Shuffletown," she said, sharing a wonderful secret. Her eyes sparkled with more than happiness. They reflected compassion from a wellspring of love deep within her. Not carnal love, but the other kind, a sort of radiant goodness. Xan felt more attracted to her than ever, and yet, conversely, he was caught up in a backwash of dismay. Her own practice! As an obstetrician, he didn't want to believe it.

He forced himself to keep his face blank. "Tell me about it," he said, knowing with an appalling certainty that the more he heard, the less he'd like it.

Her words tumbled over one another like the flow of a freshening brook. "I want to start my own clinic for expectant mothers, a place where they can learn good nutrition and exercise. And then I'll be able to attend them in their own homes when they give birth, too. You know, Xan, I think I've found the place where I'm really needed, where I can use my skills in midwifery to truly make a difference in people's lives."

Xan managed through sheer willpower to keep his expression neutral. She didn't know, couldn't know, but every word she uttered hit him in the gut, and hard.

"I'm hoping to find an able assistant to train to be a midwife," Maura went on, warming to her subject but oblivious to Xan's pain. The whole time she was talking, all Xan could think about was how in the world he was going to tell her that as an obstetrician he regarded her attempts to set up a Shuffletown practice in midwifery as sheer effrontery, not to mention detrimental to the public good. And that despite her high-flying notions, she'd better find some place other than Shuffletown to practice midwifery.

The fried chicken arrived along with fresh biscuits and gravy, and she devoured the food eagerly. Further thought was impossible for Xan. She'd dashed his hopes about them as a couple, threatened his livelihood, and brought unwelcome competition for the Quinby Hospital, all in one fell swoop. It was all he could do to nibble on one skinny chicken leg, and the biscuits dried up his mouth like so much dust.

"So what do you think?" she finally asked him, halting her rhythmic and expressive flow of words.

"I think," he said abruptly, standing up and pulling his wallet out of his pocket, "that we'd better get you home."

Maura stopped eating and blotted her mouth with

the tiny paper napkin. What was happening? She was barely through eating, and Xan was so gruff, and his expression had gone all stony and unreadable. He had hardly eaten anything on his plate, even though the food was delicious.

"Xan?" she said, staring up at him. Suddenly she knew what had gone wrong. No matter how admiring he had been of her expertise in delivering Annie's baby, despite his kindness, he was like all the rest of the doctors she'd ever known. He felt threatened. She had been a fool to talk on and on about her practice in midwifery, and even more of a fool to entertain the notion that he would be willing to be her supervising physician.

His expression softened when he read the impact of her disappointment on her pale face. He couldn't bear to look at her. "I'll pay the check," he said, and he strode away from her toward the cash register.

Maura slid across the slick red plastic seat and followed Xan to the door. He held it open for her, avoiding her eyes, and she followed him as he stalked to the Honda. "Here," he said, thrusting the gold-flecked helmet at her. "Put this on."

She looked mutely up at him, and the confusion in her eyes stopped him cold. He didn't like acting this way; he had loved her earnestness back there in the restaurant and the way she had so vivaciously shared with him the things that were important to her.

But there wasn't any way he could fit her into his life if she insisted upon this folly, this practice in midwifery. And he, who had never wanted to arrange his life around any serious relationship with a woman, whose emotions were bound up in his dedication to his profession, had set his heart on having her in his life. He hadn't known how much until he'd realized it was impossible.

"If you'd rather not take me home," she said, "I could call Don or Kathleen to come and get me." She was gazing up at him with those velvet-brown eyes, and more than anything he wanted to burrow into them and be enfolded in their softness.

Xan ran a hand through his hair, wishing he were running it through hers. He shook his head. "Don't be ridiculous," he said. "I'm taking you home."

He held the Honda steady as she swung one long leg over the seat. She felt too constrained to wrap her arms around him as he gunned the engine and they swooped out of the parking lot. Instead she balanced herself by settling one hand on either side of his waist above his trim hips, trying to remain impervious to his effect on her. Thank goodness there wasn't any way for him to know the way she reacted to him. She wasn't used to being around men, she thought tremulously. And it showed.

After a ride remarkable only for the tension stretched between them so tautly that Maura dared not speak, Xan pulled the motorcycle up in front of Don and Kathleen's house. The Teoway Island home of the O'Malleys was a magnificent house, all weathered wood and soaring angles, with wide smoked-glass windows overlooking the marsh. Architecturally, the structure was at one with its surroundings, looking not at all out of place amid the pines and hickories and sweet gums; these had not been cut down to make room for a lawn but were allowed to grow unimpeded in their natural state.

Xan switched off the Honda. The night immediately seemed too quiet. They sat for a moment in silence until they began to hear the sounds of a giant bullfrog in the marsh and then the soft cacophony of the other night creatures of wetlands and forest as they joined in. It was obvious to both of them that each was waiting for the other to make the first move.

Maura slid from her seat. Xan did, too. "Looks like no one is home," commented Xan. His words sounded empty, and they both knew that it was a hollow remark, uttered to fill up the space between them.

"Don and Kathleen often go out at night," Maura said, knowing even as she spoke the words that this was nothing Xan didn't already know.

Xan made no move to remove her midwife's kit from his saddlebag. "Don't you go out with them?" he asked a bit sharply.

Maura shook her head. "No. I'm not much into socializing." She had the craziest impulse to tell him how the very idea of a party frightened her, how she'd never learned how to dance, how she wouldn't have the nerve to drink a cocktail. She cast her eyes down. That at least was a reaction that came almost second nature.

She waited for him to open his saddlebag, but he didn't. "I'll need my things," she said.

"Oh, of course," he said, and he unbuckled the saddlebag, fumbling in the dark, and removed her leather bag. As she took it from him, their fingers brushed, and his touch fluttered through her, warm as the night wind.

Silently he walked her to the door of the house. Only a single porch spotlight was lit in this modern house of angles and glass, the light picking out the roughness of the weathered cypress boards and glinting on the wide glass expanses of the windows.

She turned to him in the glare of the spotlight, and a glance at his face arrested all thought. His eyes pulled her into their depths, treating her to a glimpse of the man's underlying sensuality, the passion beneath the smooth outer veneer. He wasn't trying to hide it, and yet she sensed a new reserve in his attitude toward her.

"I'll see that you get your van back tomorrow," he said, standing so close that she could feel his breath whiffle against her cheek with each word he spoke.

She tried to smile, but she was suddenly so tired. "Thank you for everything," she told him, her voice low.

The smoldering in his eyes pierced the veil of her self-consciousness, and in that breathtaking moment Maura knew he had thrown aside his reserve and was going to kiss her. Like a child frightened of the unknown, she whirled quickly, running, but he was too quick for her.

His hands were hot against her skin, his arms viselike as he wrenched her around to face him. The current that passed from him to her was electric, passionate. Maura had no time to voice even a token protest as his lips crushed hers in a kiss that took possession of her mouth in a way she had never dreamed a kiss could do.

Releasing her mouth but not her body, Xan pressed her back into the shadowed alcove of the door, using his lean hard length to pin her against the rough siding so she couldn't move. "I've been wanting to do this ever since I saw you making something beautiful out of a life's beginning back in Annie Bodkin's house," he said unsteadily. "You were so lovely—you *are* so lovely. The loveliest—" but he didn't finish his sentence. Instead he lowered his lips to hers, gently this time, and drew her into a kiss so absorbing and so deeply passionate that she wanted to die from the exquisite sensation of it. His tongue burned against her lips, and without another thought she opened to him, only distantly aware of his body, every surging muscle of it, imprisoning her against the wall.

Sweetly and insistently his hand skimmed its way upward and cupped the lush curve of her breast over her thin blouse, lifting the full weight of her breast in his hand so that for one wild moment she felt owned by him and wanted to yield to him totally and completely. When he sensed her impassioned response to his caress, he slowly trailed his tongue down the full length of her tender throat, breathing deeply of the scent of her in the shadowed hollow above the neckline of her garment.

But this is insane, she thought in protest, struggling to regain control of herself. She threw her head back, breathing deeply of the night air damp and fragrant of the marsh, but that only aligned her breasts closer to his seeking lips. When he lifted her voluptuous breast to his mouth, contouring the shape of her with his gentle knowing fingers, she gasped.

"Maura," he whispered, and she cradled his bowed head in her arms, pressing his moist lips to her aching breast even as she knew she must stop. "I can't believe you don't want this. You're melting in my arms." His breath was hot through her clothing, and his mouth left a damp spot there that clung to her skin.

She let her arms go limp and dropped them to her sides. "I'm not ready," she told him evasively, the words a mere whisper. *Nor will you ever be,* taunted a voice inside her.

He lifted his head and moved slightly away from her, his dark eyes acknowledging her right to halt the proceedings. "I," he told her, his lips full with passion, his voice heavy with emotion, "am ready whenever you are."

She lifted her chin, willing herself to be strong in the face of his all-too-persuasive desire. "I have to go in now," she said, the formal tone of her voice injecting a barrier between them. "It's really very late."

He stared at her for a moment, the moonlight glinting in the depths of his eyes—heavy-lidded now, their lids weighed by the force of his passion. "On the contrary," he said slowly, meaningfully. "For us, it's very early."

His words left no doubt in her mind that he intended to see her again, and she knew that seeing him again would interfere with her achieving her goals here. Already her brain fought her purely physical desire to understand even more about him than she already knew, to know how her body would join itself to the curves and angles of his, what it would be like to gentle his head upon her breasts.

She fumbled behind her until her hand found the doorknob, and still holding his eyes so full of longing, she slipped inside the house and closed the door. She leaned her forehead against it as Xan walked away. The rhythm of her pulse surged in her ears.

Xan, driving down the deserted street, wondered how long it would take before Maura was ready for what he was sure she wanted. He had known many women in his lifetime, but he had never been so fascinated by any one woman in his entire life. He was totally captivated by her naturalness, a quality that intrigued him because it didn't seem to fit in with the indefinable mystery about her. One thing for sure, she was one woman he meant to have.

Maura finally tiptoed down the long glass-windowed hallway to the guest room, where she stood staring at herself in the mirror, barely breathing and wondering how she could look like the same person when she didn't feel like the same person. All in all, she supposed it wasn't unusual that she felt so different. Xan's kisses had exposed a lustful facet of her personality that she had never known existed.

Which wasn't really surprising when she considered that she hadn't been kissed since she was eighteen years old.

Chapter Four

There should be some sort of reentry cram course to
the world for ex-nuns, thought Maura. A school
where you could go to learn about all the things you
didn't learn in the convent. With courses in such dis-
ciplines as "Coping with Day-to-Day Problems." In
"Figuring Out How to Spend the Rest of Your Life."
"Balancing a Checkbook." And of course "Men." Or
maybe that one should be titled "Love." No, "Men"
would be better. After all, men didn't necessarily
mean love. What *men* all too often meant was sex,
and you could have that without love. She'd just, in
her breathless clinch with Xan, figured that out for
herself. Chalk up a point for Sister Maura. Or, she
reminded herself ruefully, ex-Sister Maura.

The fact that Kathleen and Don were not home was
a huge relief. As good Catholics, her sister and
brother-in-law were still in shock over Maura's sudden departure from the nursing order of nuns to
which she'd belonged for ten years. Although she had
tried to answer all their questions honestly, Maura

was embarrassed to find that they regarded her warily,
as they would someone who had somehow unexpectedly figured out a way to come back from the dead.
Her reinvolvement with the world was something
they had no idea how to help her accomplish. Mostly
they stood back in awestruck surprise and let Maura
proceed at her own pace. Her choices were not always
what theirs would have been.

Kathleen and Don had thought of her as Sister
Maura, their pious relative in California, for so long
that it was hard for them to picture her in any other
kind of life. That was why Maura never felt that she
actually managed to communicate in any real, deep-
down way with them, and so she was singularly glad
that she didn't have to explain her late-night arrival tonight astride the back of a blue Honda with Xan Copeland. It was another thing they probably wouldn't
understand.

She stripped off her clothes while her bath ran. On
impulse she picked up a bottle of Kathleen's pink
Vitabath and squeezed a larger-than-necessary dollop
into the swirling water. When the huge sunken tub
was full, she sank into the froth and contemplated her
own bodily comfort. It was okay, she reminded herself, for a body to feel good. The notion that bodies
were supposed to feel good was one of the first ideas
to have been trained out of her when she entered the
novitiate.

From a nun's life to a normal life—was the transi-
tion going to go smoothly? When she fled from Xan
Copeland's office today, ran right out of the examin-

ing room, she hadn't felt confident about returning to the real world at all. And Xan's kisses—not to mention his very sensual presence—had left her in a quandary about her feelings for men. The one thing that was going to help her bridge the gap to normality was her work, her calling. Her midwifery. It was the one constant in her life.

Maura had never dreamed when she set out this morning that she would end up officiating at a birthing. A fond smile touched her lips as she thought of Annie's new son. He had been a vigorous newborn and, above all, healthy. That was the important thing, and it was that fact that gave her the most satisfaction of all. Annie had sleepily insisted, just before Maura left, that she was going to name her son Maurice, in honor of Maura.

Annie's gratitude put her in mind of the appreciative ghetto families she had served in California. They had been poor, too, as poor as the Bodkins, but theirs had been a different life-style. Most of the families in the ghetto surrounding the convent and the hospital it had served had been black or Hispanic, and they had welcomed Maura's skillful midwife's hands with their hearts. She had moved around the neighborhood with ease and spirit, able to call even the leaders of the toughest youth gangs by name. She'd never felt out of place or afraid, even as the neighborhood grew increasingly run-down and crime-ridden. Even the more frequent attacks on lone women didn't scare her.

Ah, but it had been just such an attack that had ended her midwifery practice in that neighborhood.

Would she fear for her safety here, among the Shuffletown people? She didn't think she would. She hadn't before, even after what had happened to Sister Angela.

She closed her eyes against the memories, sinking even deeper into the warm soothing water. She must have dozed off in the tub because the bubbles had nearly all dissolved when she opened her eyes and heard Kathleen's muffled laughter as she and Don tiptoed down the hallway toward the master bedroom.

Maura caught Kathleen's words: "Do you think she's asleep?" And then Don whispered, but not low enough, "I hope so. Or she's going to witness the world's greatest seduction. You look marvelous in that dress, but you'll look even better out of it."

The door to Kathleen and Don's room closed with a click, and as she lay back in the tub Maura could hear Kathleen's low laughter. Afraid to move, afraid of noisily swishing the water as she stood up, Maura remained motionless. She didn't want to interrupt their privacy, and she felt somehow very much alone in those moments.

Then she heard more laughter, arrested suddenly by an appreciative moan, and she closed her eyes, embarrassed at her role as eavesdropper. When she heard no more sounds from the direction of Kathleen and Don's bedroom, she stood as quietly as she could and stopped the runnels of water from dripping by wrapping a giant bath sheet around her.

Maura wondered how it would be to be like Kathleen and Don, married. Knowing there'd always be

someone to talk with about your own concerns, someone in your corner even when the rest of the world
was hostile or unfeeling. It was a mind-set foreign to
Maura, marriage never before having been one of her
options.

She dried herself completely and put on her plain
blue cotton pajamas, then crawled into the big king-
size bed in the guest room. She sprawled out, letting
her long legs take up as much room as they wanted.
This, she thought, hands clasped behind her head as
she luxuriated in her sole occupancy of the huge mattress, was something married people couldn't enjoy. It
was wonderful to know you had plenty of room to
stretch tired muscles without hitting your kneecap
against someone else's hard shinbone.

And then, before the smile completely left her
face, she fell fast asleep.

IN THEIR ROOM, Kathleen and Don lay entwined in
each other's arms. "It's something I really want to
do," Kathleen told her husband, tracing one of his
bushy blond eyebrows with an oval fingernail enam-
eled in a shade called Coppery Glaze. "Helping Maura
means a lot to me. You know that."

"I know. What I can't fathom is how you could
bear to see her work in Shuffletown. The place gives
me the shudders." Don spoke lazily, but he meant
what he said. The moneyed youngest son of a wealthy
Boston Irish family, he was used to living well and
luxuriously, and he didn't like to work too hard. This
job as a tennis pro was exactly right for him—playing

tennis in the warm Teoway sunshine during the day, attending parties with his lovely wife at night. Why would anyone—especially his sister-in-law Maura— want to work amid the poor and illiterate of Shuffletown?

Kathleen sighed and settled her head into her husband's shoulder. "It's what Maura wants. It's what she's cut out to do, if only you'd see it. Burning with the longing to help the impoverished masses, that's our Maura. You'd have to have grown up with us to understand this drive that she has, I guess."

He kissed her temple. "If it will make you happy, and if it will make Maura happy, I'll see that she gets the money. The O'Malley Family Foundation can set up a grant or a trust or whatever it takes. Then Maura can minister to all the pregnant women in Shuffletown and points north, south, east and west, if she likes."

"You mean it?" Her eyes flew to his. "Just as easily as that?"

"Sure," he said, gazing at her with his own special brand of loving adoration. "Just as easily as that."

Kathleen closed her eyes with a happy sigh. "Wake me when you get up in the morning," she murmured into the soft blond hair on Don's chest. She'd get up early and surprise Maura with the news about the O'Malley Family Foundation grant. She couldn't think of anything that would please her sister more.

MAURA ROSE with the sun. She scrubbed her face with soap and water and brushed her thick hair until it hung instead of snarled in what her mother used to call rat's nests. Pulling on her housecoat over her pajamas, she hurried to the kitchen. So far she was the only one up, so she plugged in the coffeepot for Kathleen and Don, although she never drank coffee herself.

"Good morning," said Kathleen agreeably as she swept into the kitchen wearing an expensive negligee of dusty-rose chiffon with flowing sleeves bordered in maribou. It was a striking contrast to Maura's own worn housecoat. Otherwise, the sisters resembled each other greatly, although Maura was taller than Kathleen and the planes of her face were less rounded. They could have been twins, although at twenty-six Kathleen was the younger by two years.

"I hope you didn't get up just because of me," protested Maura.

"Oh, no. Don has an early tennis game this morning. And besides, I have wonderful news!" Kathleen poured herself a cup of the freshly made coffee and sat down at the table beside Maura, grinning as though she had swallowed the proverbial canary and its feathers were tickling her throat.

"Well, don't tell me, make me suffer," said Maura dryly.

Kathleen's eyes danced. She'd never been good at keeping secrets. "What if I told you that your money problems are over? That you'll be able to set up your practice as a midwife in Shuffletown without worrying about the financial end of it?"

Maura started. "I'd say you'd lost your mind," she said.

Don came into the kitchen, dressed in his tennis whites, which contrasted with his deep tan and set off his sandy blond hair and mustache. He dropped a kiss on the top of his wife's head and went to pour his own cup of coffee.

"I was just telling Maura that she won't have to worry about financing her birth center," said Kathleen.

"And I was just saying that she'd lost her mind," said Maura.

"My wife may have lost her mind, but it's true," he told Maura with a grin that twitched his mustache upward at the ends. "I'll arrange for the O'Malley Family Foundation to finance your venture. No strings attached."

Maura's jaw dropped. She had never hoped for anything like this, had never dreamed that such a thing was possible. "Don?" she said, her voice quavering. "You're not joking?"

"Would I joke about a project so near and dear to your heart that you've scarcely stopped talking about it ever since the first time you drove that broken-down old van of yours through Shuffletown?" Don was eyeing her with amusement.

"So, sister mine, all you have to do is find a place of business and *voilà*! Shuffletown has its very own practicing midwife." Kathleen's face shone with satisfaction.

Maura was out of her chair in a second, embracing her sister first and then hugging Don. "Oh, thank you!" she exclaimed, happy tears springing to her eyes.

"And now," said Kathleen, "tell us your plans. I'm sure, knowing you, that you've made them—lots of them."

Maura blinked the dampness away. "Well, first I'm going to have to find a place suitable for my birth center. I've been thinking about one of the old houses in Shuffletown, one with a lot of rooms that can be converted to examining rooms and so forth." Then she frowned. "I'd go out looking for such a place first thing this morning if I had my van."

"You don't have your van?" said Kathleen, looking puzzled. "I hadn't realized that it was gone."

"It isn't," said Don, joining them at the table. "It's parked right where it always is, beside that stand of palmettos. I saw it when I went out to look for the morning paper."

"You're sure?" said Maura, taken aback.

"Of course I'm sure. I'd know that heap anywhere. When you get the O'Malley grant, how about buying a new van? Or at least having the old one painted?" Don grinned at her affectionately.

With a peculiar look on her face, Maura went to the window. Sure enough, there was her van parked in its usual place. "He must have brought it back early," she said.

"Who? And what was wrong with it?"

"Oh, the uncooperative old thing broke down again, this time on the Shuffletown highway, and it was at the garage being repaired," she said. "I'm surprised to have it back so soon, that's all. Now that it's here, I might as well get busy and try to find a suitable location for my birth center." And she beat a hasty retreat before Kathleen and Don could ask any more unwelcome questions. And before Maura could answer the "who" part of the questions they'd already asked.

All the time that she was dressing, Maura wondered about Xan. Had he delivered the van this morning himself? When? And how much money did she owe the garage, anyway?

She wished she had thought to bring up all relevant questions last night, but it was a night definitely not to be remembered for its overabundance of rational thought. She could at least have asked Xan for his home phone number.

Of course she could reach him at his office. That, however, didn't seem like a course she wanted to take after her sudden leave-taking yesterday afternoon. The sweet-faced office nurse might very well hang up on her, sweet face or not.

"Maura?" Kathleen knocked lightly on the open guest-room door.

"You don't have to tap so politely," Maura informed her sister with a smile. "Remember when we were kids? You barged right into my room whenever you wanted, no matter what I was doing."

"Barging in on a big sister is a little sister's prerogative. But we aren't kids anymore," Kathleen reminded her, looking fondly at Maura. "You look wonderful in that knit two-piece thing you're wearing. The jade green looks marvelous against your hair."

"This suit was yours," Maura told her. "Don't you remember giving it to me? That's probably why it looks good, if it does. Our hair is practically the same shade." She somehow felt that she had to make excuses for her wholesome good looks. Nuns were supposed to remain humble.

Kathleen looked at the suit again. It clung ever so gracefully to Maura's curvy figure, and Maura was taller than Kathleen, so the two-piece effect was perfect for her. It annoyed her that Maura was so self-effacing about her natural beauty. "Maura, you must learn to accept compliments," she said sharply. At Maura's flustered look Kathleen went on, more gently this time. "That suit looks much better on you than it ever did on me. And you do need clothes, you know. When can we go shopping?" Kathleen, with her love of fashion, was forever trying to organize a shopping trip.

Maura smiled and shook her head. "I hate shopping, and besides, the only clothes I'll need for what I'm going to be doing is a good supply of clean smocks and a leotard or two for teaching pregnant women their exercises. Give up on me, Kath. I'm not going to stay here with Don and you on Teoway Island, you know, even though you're a most accommodating host and hostess."

Kathleen's eyebrows flew up in alarm. "You're not? Where are you going?"

"I'm going to find a place to live in Shuffletown. No, don't look so horrified. It's important to me to live among the people with whom I'm working."

"Maura—" Kathleen was clearly about to protest.

"Don't Maura me," said Maura, kissing her sister swiftly on the cheek. "And don't expect me back any time soon. I have no idea how long this project of finding a home for my birth center will take."

"I was about to ask you to go with me to a luncheon and my garden-club meeting," said Kathleen, impatient with Maura's cheerful unwillingness to become a part of normal Teoway Island society.

"You know such frivolity is not my idea of an afternoon of fun," chided Maura, sweeping her midwife's bag off the chair where she had tossed it last night. She blew Kathleen a kiss. "See you later," she said, breezing out of the room.

"Good luck," Kathleen called bemusedly after her sister. Frivolity! She couldn't wait to repeat this conversation to Don. The very activities Maura considered frivolous were considered normal everyday worthwhile pastimes for Teoway Island women. Don would consider Maura's reluctance to get involved as just another attempt by his nonconformist sister-in-law to forsake worldly glory. Which, Kathleen thought, was all very well and good. But certainly this was an unrealistic attitude in the real world to which Maura had returned.

As Maura stepped outside into the morning air, its softness freshened by a wispy wind from the nearby ocean, she had no such thoughts on her mind. The most important thing this morning was to first figure out the situation with her van.

The key hung from the van's ignition. Maura

checked the space above the visor in case Xan had left a note or a bill; there was nothing. As a matter of habit, she opened her midwife's bag for a routine check of the contents.

And it wasn't her midwife's bag.

It was a medical bag, all right. Black leather on the outside, stethoscope on the inside. And other objects, too, but they weren't her objects. This was a doctor's bag.

Stunned, she looked at the outside of the bag. It could have passed for her own. She recalled last night, with Xan fumbling with his motorcycle saddlebag in the dark and pulling out her bag. He had put her bag in his saddlebag at the Bodkins' place, she remembered it clearly. It was when she had seen the twin moons in his eyes.

This medical bag must have been in his saddlebag then; in his right-hand saddlebag. He had put hers in the left.

He had given her the wrong bag. And that meant that he must have hers! She rummaged through the bag. Yes, here was his card, ALEXANDER COPELAND. M.D. Xan would be needing the bag, and she should see that he got it.

She drove first to the Shuffletown business district and bought a bed board to slide beneath the sagging mattress of Annie Bodkin's bed. When she pulled her van up in front of the old shack, Cindy came dancing outside to escort her inside.

"Little Maurice is just fine," Annie assured her. Annie was sitting up in bed looking pert and pleased.

Quickly Maura checked the baby, and then she checked Annie. Annie was recovering, and the baby was alert and energetic.

Maura and Cindy unloaded the bed board from the back of the van, Maura cursing the dress she wore, wishing she had decided to wear her usual blue jeans instead. "The bed board is going to keep you from getting a backache," she told Annie as she remade the bed.

"Sure do thank you," Annie said gratefully. "I've got to get back on my feet soon. I want to find a job."

Ascertaining that Annie had worked as a maid before her pregnancy, Maura promised to mention to Kathleen that Annie was looking for work. Kathleen might have some friends on Teoway Island who were looking for a maid.

"Anything I can ever do for you, just let me know," Annie told her gratefully.

"You can do me a favor," she told Annie as she deftly started a nutritious stew bubbling on a back burner of the old wood stove. "I want to open a birth center, where I can coach pregnant women on nutrition and exercise and help them to have their babies at home if they choose, just the way you did yesterday. I need a large house or office. Do you know of one?"

Annie thought for a moment. "There's a big old farmhouse about two miles from here," she told Maura. "I think it's for rent. There's a lady at the real estate agency down the road who might be able to tell you something about it."

And so, after pulling off the borrowed apron and instructing Cindy in the completion of the stew, Maura went straight to the real estate office. There she met a plump and interested woman named Grace Murdock, who took her idea for a birth center to heart and said, "Come on, I'll show you that farmhouse right now. It sounds perfect for your birth center." Maura left her van parked beneath a shady and accommodating oak tree in the agency parking lot and got into Grace's compact blue car.

Grace, a lively and talkative lady, drove her Chevette down the bumpy unpaved road, explaining as she clung gamely to the vibrating steering wheel. "It's a farmhouse without its own farm. The land around it has been bought by developers, who are waiting until financial conditions are more favorable before they do any developing. They've rented out the land, so cotton fields run right up to the house, but that may not bother you. For most people, the place is too far out in the country."

"I like the country," Maura assured her, remembering her days in the ghetto surrounding the convent.

The farmhouse that would become the McNeill Birth Center turned out to be ideally suited to Maura's needs. The house was bordered on three sides by a porch, which put Maura in mind of nothing so much as a wide, comfortable lap. The front yard was amply shaded by six immense pecan trees inhabited by a family of friendly chattering squirrels.

"It's perfect," said Maura, who had been captivated by the big, sunny rooms. They drove back to the office immediately, and Maura went inside and waited while the lease was prepared. She signed it on the spot.

She hurried back outside with her head full of plans. She climbed into her van, ideas dancing an Irish jig through her mind. She'd go back to Teoway and take a pad and paper out on the beautiful Teoway Island beach, find some solitary spot where she could make lists of the things she'd need and decide on the best way to divide up the space available into a lab and exercise and examining rooms.

Then her eyes fell on Xan's medical bag. What she should do immediately was track him down and exchange bags with him. But remembering her breathless passion of the night before, she'd feel uncomfortable doing that. She was sure that by this time Xan knew he had her bag. He'd seek her out, because he needed his bag more than she needed hers right now. She'd explain the situation to Kathleen the best she could, and when Xan called, she'd let Kathleen, who was unfailingly adept in awkward social situations, make the exchange. That was the best way to handle it, and it would save Maura the embarrassment, after last night, of seeing Xan again.

In a hurry to get to the cool beach, Maura drove as fast as the speed limit allowed down the Shuffletown highway toward Teoway Island, pausing briefly as the old sideways-swinging drawbridge swung closed after letting a boat pass, then turning quickly into the Teoway Island entrance, magnificently landscaped with showy red and yellow zinnias.

The temperamental brakes locked as she brought the van to a stop under the palmetto trees at the side of the O'Malleys' driveway, sending Xan's medical bag rocketing between the two separate front seats.

"Hey," said a sleepy voice from the nether regions of the van, "a fellow can hardly sleep while you're driving so dangerously. I wish you'd learn to put on your brakes as carefully as you deliver babies."

Incredulously she swiveled in her seat. Her eyes met those of an indignant Xan Copeland, who was struggling to sit up on the cot in the back of her van and quite obviously stifling the urge to yawn. Judging from the way his hair fell so loosely over his forehead and from the half-staff look of his eyelids, he was just waking up from a midday nap.

Chapter Five

"I won't ask you the obvious question," she said when she was able to overcome her amazement at finding him there.

"Go ahead," he urged. Now he stood and lurched toward the front of the van, settling himself on the seat opposite her. His eyes twinkled mischievously.

"Well, then," she went on, "suppose you tell me why you're sleeping in my van."

"Because after I brought you home last night, I was called out to deliver a baby, and I didn't get much sleep. And because I found out I had a bag that didn't belong to me, which meant that you had mine. I saw your van in the real estate agency parking lot after I left my office at noon, and I thought I'd wait for you to return so we could exchange bags. I remembered you had a cot in here, so I couldn't resist the chance to nod off for a few minutes. How was I to know that you'd abduct me?"

"Abduct you?" sputtered Maura.

"Yes. It's a good thing it's my regular afternoon off, or my office staff would be incensed. They don't like it when I disappear without a trace. By the way, what are you doing this afternoon?"

"I'm going to the beach. Here, take your bag. I don't suppose you have mine handy?"

"Indeed I do. I put it at the foot of the cot." He paused. "Say, I'm going to the beach, too. I'll wait for you on the boardwalk. Can you be there in fifteen minutes?"

She fixed him with an exasperated look. "Xan, I have some serious thinking to do. I don't want to share my time with anyone, I just want to be alone."

"Antisocial, aren't you? And after I went out of my way to help you yesterday, too. How's the van running?"

"It's running beautifully, thank you. And I really appreciate everything you did. How much was the garage bill? I'll write you a check."

"There's no bill. It was only a broken fan belt. If you want to even things up, all you have to do is meet me at the beach. I'll try not to interfere with your mental processes. You can be as alone as you like. Just let me sit and look at you." He was flirting with her; she knew that.

"Xan, I don't see how I could possibly think things through if you're there," she protested.

"I'm only proposing adding myself to you for an hour or two, nothing heavy. What do you have to think about, anyway?"

"Setting up my practice in midwifery," she said in

her own direct way, figuring that he wouldn't press her after that.

"Good," he said. "That's exactly what I want to talk to you about."

This surprised her. "Honestly?"

"Yes. Let's go to the beach together. It'd be a chance for us to talk." He had dropped the flirtation; now he was so sincere that she considered it. "There are some things that you should understand before you go ahead with these plans of yours," he insisted.

"It's too late for you to change my mind. I'm going to establish a practice in midwifery in Shuffletown no matter what. I have financing and I've signed a lease."

His heart plummeted. Still, maybe it wasn't really too late. "Then you'd better hear what I have to say about the Shuffletown community and why I know I'm right when I tell you that women are better off with hospital births."

If he had thrown down a gauntlet, it couldn't have been more of a challenge. And if he wanted to tell her why he was in favor of hospital births, she'd have a chance to refute his beliefs with her own impassioned defense of home births. "All right," she said. "I'll meet you on the boardwalk in fifteen minutes."

Xan's smile showed his relief, but there was an underlying gravity, too. "It's a deal."

"Can I drive you home?"

He shook his head. "I live on the ocean side of the island. It's only about a five-minute jog. Anyway, you'd better save your van for more vital transportation problems."

"Let's hope it's not going to break down anymore. And here, you might as well take this," she said, handing his bag over to him.

He got out of the van. "I'm glad to get it back," he told her, looking up at her through the window. "I'm sure I'd look ridiculous in that smock you wear." His eyes sought and held hers as they both grinned.

He'd disarmed her totally. She couldn't stay annoyed with him, she thought helplessly to herself as she let herself into the house. It would be better if she could. For she knew, even if he didn't, that there was no future for the two of them, at least not in a traditional, romantic man—woman relationship. She wasn't going to let personal feelings get in the way of her mission here. She'd already proved unworthy of her vocation and her order. But she wasn't going to prove unworthy of the poor people who needed her, ever again. Not even for Xan Copeland.

AFTER A FEW MOMENTS' thoughtful hesitation in front of her closet, Maura pulled out the black swimsuit Kathleen had bought for her. Maura had finally consented to owning the black one-piece tube because she had thought it would look sedate.

However, combined with her shape and her tawny coloring, it made her look slinky and voluptuous, with a decidedly seductive effect. In her hurry, she didn't stop to put on a cover-up, and she was totally unaware of her allure as she hurried along the wooden walk across the dunes with her own special flowing walk, looking for Xan.

Xan was waiting for her, leaning against the rough railing of the platform beside the steps to the beach and gazing out over the wide expanse of sand. The ocean was calm today, but the flat sea bottom extended far out, creating waves that rolled inward upon themselves at a steady pace, one after the other.

Maura caught her breath when she saw Xan. He exuded maleness by simply standing there, his hair blowing in the wind. He wore a narrow red band of a swimsuit, and its taut outlines left little to the imagination. His clothes had done nothing to show off his long muscles, his golden tan, his sinewy legs. Maura had a flashing unbidden vision of her own long legs smoothly intertwined with his beneath cool white sheets, and she never thought once about hitting her kneecap against his shinbone. Their touching would be too perfect for that, too natural...and then she brought herself up short. What she was thinking of was an invasion of her private space, and even, eventually, an invasion of her body! She couldn't even imagine such a process, at least not in connection with herself.

He had known she would look gorgeous in a swimsuit, but still he was surprised. He had found beauty in the angular planes of her face and in her hair, flickering now like flames in the afternoon sunlight. He hadn't realized that her waist was tiny, so tiny that he could probably span it with his two hands, and it curved outward so beautifully into her hips that she seemed sculpted, created by an artist whose eye for proportion was not just practiced but inspired.

"I thought we could walk down the beach for a while," he said in greeting. He shouldered a big blanket that he had tossed across the railing, his eyes gleaming for a moment before he lowered their lids.

"All right," she said, following him down the stairs to the sand.

Summer was a busy time on Teoway, the season when families and their children arrived to spend time and plenty of money on a vacation to rival any for food and facilities and just plain fun. There were bicycle trails through the woods and an authentic old mansion to explore, but the wide sandy beach was by far the most popular recreation area. However, the crush of people thinned out considerably as Maura and Xan strolled toward the deserted southernmost end of the ten-mile-long island.

"Tell me about yourself," Xan said suddenly when they had left everyone else behind.

This startled her. She hadn't expected to be spotlighted. "What do you want to know?" she hedged.

"Where you were born, that sort of thing. Your background. All of it." He gazed down at her, and she felt a tug of remembrance as his eyes met hers. They looked misty, and she knew he was thinking about last night.

"I was born in Chicago," she said, staring resolutely ahead.

"Irish, I'm sure," he prodded.

"Yes, and Kathleen and I grew up Irish-American with all that our Irishness implied," she said.

"And what did it imply?" he asked curiously. His

own background was old-family Charleston; he could scarcely imagine growing up any other way.

"Big parties with green beer flowing freely on St. Patrick's Day, parochial schools, and my first communion in St. Bridget's Roman Catholic Church, with me wearing the white communion dress when it was new, and Kathleen complaining about the yellowed hand-me-down when she had to wear it two years later for her own first communion."

"Go on," he encouraged.

"We always ate steaming hot oatmeal on cold Chicago winter mornings, because McNeills always eat oatmeal in the winter. We'd go as a family to confession every Saturday night, and then Dad would take us all to Feeney's ice cream parlor for peppermint ice cream afterward. Oh, there are lots of memories. I like thinking about those days, even though it seems very long ago."

"Your mother, what was she like?" He couldn't help asking questions; in his fascination with her, he had to know everything, absolutely everything about her.

"Mother was Fiona Grady, and she married Chicago's most confirmed bachelor John McNeill against everyone's advice when she was eighteen. She tamed him, they say. I was born a year later, and Kathleen two years after that. We would have undoubtedly been a big family if Mother hadn't come down with what was always referred to in whispers as 'female trouble' and had an operation." Maura remembered the operation; she'd been four years old at the time and had been frightened at her mother's white, pinched face when she came home from the hospital.

But Fiona had recovered, and she had gone on to preside over a family that was famous throughout their neighborhood for its individualism. Instead of belonging to the altar society and learning how to starch and iron the altar cloths to the priest's satisfaction, Fiona surprised everyone by joining the civil rights movement before it was fashionable to do so. The cause took up every spare moment and then some, but Maura and Kathleen grew used to her frequent absences, and Maura learned at a surprisingly early age to cook the family oatmeal without lumps, a technique Fiona had still not managed to perfect.

Maura was explaining just how to cook smooth oatmeal when she and Xan came upon a driftwood log, its surface gray and shiny, protruding from the sand. Xan led Maura to it. He spread the blanket out for them in front of it, and after a moment's hesitation she sat down beside him.

"Don't stop talking," he urged, thinking that he loved to watch the expressions on her face as they provided the backdrop for the mellifluous flow of her words. "Tell me about your father."

"Oh, he's a big burly man who loves my mother and us and hunting, in that order." She laughed a bit. "Right now he and Mother are on a backpacking trip in Alaska. It was Mother's retirement present to Dad."

"Are you close to your father?"

Maura nodded. "We're all close. But my father— well, the thing about him that affected me most in terms of my life was that when I was a child he would disappear for weeks into the Michigan north woods or the wilds of Canada to hunt bear or moose or ducks, and when he arrived home with his trophies I'd be sickened by the thought of so much killing and throw up into the nearest receptacle." Her father's hunting expeditions left her with a loathing of hurting any live thing, a loathing that was to stay with her all her life. She didn't know why she wanted to tell this to Xan; it seemed so personal.

Xan didn't laugh or make light of her feelings. Instead he gazed at her with respect. "I'm the same way," he told her. "There's a lot of wildlife on Teoway Island, and hunting isn't allowed, although the whole island used to be a private game preserve for the very wealthy. I look at the ducks and the raccoons and the deer who brighten my life by their very presence on the island and wonder how anyone could be so cruel as to harm any one of them."

They sat watching the waves chase each other toward shore, their bodies so close that there was barely a few inches of air between them, and their thoughts so in tune that there might have been no space between them at all.

"Uncomplicated Maura," he mused, leaning on an elbow and staring up at her, one eye closed against the sun. "Move, will you? No, not that way—that's right." Now the sun was directly behind her head, backlighting her hair so that it looked as though she wore a bright golden aureole, and her head shaded his face so he didn't have to squint.

"Uncomplicated?" she said, sifting sand through her fingers. "Why do you say that?" Her eyes were on a direct line with his chest, which was covered with tightly curled dark hair tapering intriguingly toward the band of his swim trunks.

"You seem uncomplicated to me. Elemental, an earth-mother. Aren't you?"

Maura wasn't used to being talked to in this manner. It sounded fanciful to her, and she'd never been fanciful. She shrugged, smiling a bit and remembering what Kathleen had said about her learning to accept compliments, if indeed that's what this was. "The eye of the beholder," she said.

His eye beheld her as she looked now, sitting beside him. He couldn't imagine anyone being more beautiful. She wore no makeup today or yesterday, and that was good. He couldn't stand a face full of goop, all that fake stuff that made skin look like something it wasn't. He was dedicated to healing the human body, and this gave him a reverence for it, for the miracle of bone and tissue and skin. To slather layers of color and powder on such perfection seemed almost sacrilege to him. "I'm glad you don't wear makeup," he said suddenly and startlingly.

Her mouth dropped open. She closed it again. "I thought we were going to talk about important things," she protested.

"That depends on what you consider important," he pointed out. When she made no comment, he sighed and took her hand, brushing off the remaining grains of sand. It was a wide and capable hand, and he remembered how her hands had looked when they'd caught Annie's baby.

Maura wished he'd get on with the discussion, having no idea how to impel the conversation forward herself.

Xan fixed his eyes on the blue-and-white sail of a catamaran far out in the ocean. "You should have seen what Shuffletown was like when I first opened my practice in obstetrics," he told her.

"You came here straight from medical school?"

He nodded. "It was nothing but a ragtag community with no hospital, no school. Well, we still don't have a school. But I made sure we got a hospital." He turned to look at her, hard. "Maura, I begged, borrowed and stopped just short of stealing to bring the Quinby Hospital to Shuffletown. I talked the women out of having their babies in the fields. I increased the infant survival rate by five percent. It doesn't sound like much, but in a place like Shuffletown, that's practically a miracle."

"And you think my plan to bring home births to the women of Shuffletown will affect your statistics," she said.

"I don't think, I know. Maura, women in high-risk categories shouldn't give birth at home. Such women should be in hospitals where they have access to lifesaving equipment."

"I don't accept high-risk patients," she told him firmly. "I screen my patients carefully. Anyone who can't birth at home, I will send to my sponsoring physician."

His eyebrows lifted. "And just who is that sponsoring physician?"

"I was hoping it would be you." Her look was level, taking in his amazement.

"Me?" His astonished expression underscored the word.

She drew a deep breath. "I need someone to help me gain access to the hospital and the rest of the medical community. Why shouldn't it be you?"

He dropped her hand and lay back on the big blanket, closing his eyes as though they hurt. "Maura, you don't know what you're asking," he said.

"I'm talking about bringing my heart and my hands to the women of Shuffletown and to anyone else who wants my services," she said, fighting to make him understand. "Women having babies aren't sick. Most of them don't belong in a hospital. Birthing is a natural, normal process. I recognize that process and respond to it. Xan, you must comprehend what I'm saying." She was pleading now. Surely he would understand; he understood so many of the other things she'd spoken about during their short acquaintance.

Xan sat up and shook his head. "No way," he said with finality. "We don't need that kind of thing here. As a member of the board of directors of Quinby, I can't encourage you."

"I know just how women give birth in your Quinby Hospital and other places like it," said Maura, her eyes flashing. "Why, you're still using the old delivery-room procedures, not even a modern birthing room with a comfortable bed and dim lighting and an easy chair for the father! The women are regimented and very seldom given any voice in how they want the birth of their babies to proceed. I'm willing to bet that the other children in a family play no role in the birth of a new family member and that fathers play a very little part, and—"

"Wait a minute," Xan interjected indignantly. "We allow the father to be in the delivery room, provided he's had some training. We just started doing that a few years ago, and it's been a big success."

"As I said, the father plays a very little part. Do you see the father in your office when you see the expectant mother? Do you know anything about the family problems or environment?"

Xan shook his head. "You don't understand the Shuffletown people. The thing to do is to push the services of Quinby Hospital for the safety of the patients, not to encourage births in the squalor of their homes."

"Like Annie's home, you mean? It must be obvious to you that Annie would have had her baby in her home no matter what you had done. She had no way to get to prenatal checkups and no money to pay you, and I'm willing to bet she was intimidated by the thought of a doctor's office."

"You sound like a social worker, some kind of avant-garde do-gooder! What was I supposed to do, track the woman down while she was expecting her baby and drag her in for her checkups? Maura, I saw Annie Bodkin exactly twice for prenatal care, and then I never saw or heard from her again until her daughter called me from a public telephone. I'm a busy man. Do you think I could have gone out and found Annie and brought her to my office for her checkups?" His eyes bored into hers, daring her to blame him for his supposed neglect of Annie Bodkin and all the women like her.

"That is exactly what I plan to do," Maura announced triumphantly, "when I set up my practice in Shuffletown. I'll provide transportation to checkups in my clinic in my van."

"When you set up your practice in Shuffletown!" exploded Xan. "Maura, that's folly. Haven't I managed to talk some sense into you?"

"I explained to you last night just how much I'm needed in Shuffletown. Poor people have just as much right to a safe home delivery as anyone else. You're not going to change my mind. But I'm going to try my best to change yours!"

Xan's face was incredulous. "Damn it, Maura, you'd better face facts before you go ahead with this. You don't belong in Shuffletown."

"All I'm asking from you is backup care so that my patients can be admitted to Quinby Hospital if there's an emergency such as a breech birth. Is that so much to ask?"

Xan let out a sigh of exasperation and raked his fingers through his dark hair. "Yes, it is! If you botch up your deliveries, I won't take responsibility for your mistakes. Don't be ridiculous."

Seconds ticked by as Maura gazed down the beach at a flock of brown pelicans flying in formation over the water. Xan's comment about botching her deliveries had cut her to the quick. "Then I guess we're on opposite sides, Xan," she told him firmly, looking back at him but trying not to show him how much he had hurt her. "Because I'm going to establish my practice."

He had never seen anyone display so much single-minded determination She had won his admiration, too, because she honestly believed that she was right. He watched her unhappily as she unfolded herself with her own peculiar inborn grace and rose fluidly to her feet before looking down at him, her chin tilted upward.

"So it's good-bye forever?" he said with a hint of sarcasm, knowing that his tone of voice wouldn't endear him to her. He couldn't help the sarcasm, simply because he didn't know how else to react. If she had ranted uncontrollably at his position, even if she had cried, he would have known how to handle her. But this accepting serenity of hers, accentuated by the calm courage of her convictions, was something he couldn't fathom.

"Perhaps we'll see each other occasionally," she said, really hoping that this was true. She liked him. She couldn't help it. Even though he had closed one possible avenue of obtaining the necessary medical backup, she couldn't really hold it against him. Xan was the product of his training and background; she had seen doctors become defensive and angry and even abusive when confronted with the threat of midwifery.

He said nothing. A bitter feeling of frustration washed over him. He hadn't handled any of this well. He had wanted to impress her, to make her like him, and he hadn't known how. And what she did want from him, he couldn't give.

"Good-bye, Xan," she said, and she wheeled swiftly and walked away from him.

He rolled over on his stomach and let the dying rays of the afternoon sun warm his back. He rested his head on his arms and tried to think of some way to let her know that even though he disagreed with her philosophy of childbirth and wished fervently that she'd take her practice someplace else, he admired her and liked her and wanted to know her better than he did.

Chapter Six

As Maura approached the house, the throb of rock music pounded louder and louder until she felt as if some fearsome animal released by the jungle beat were about to pounce on her. She checked the address on the paper in her hand against the numerals visible in the pool of light on the porch. Yes, this was the correct address. Had she been a fool to come here?

"Of course you must come," Bonnie Trenholm had told her over the phone. Maura had discovered Bonnie, a practicing midwife working with a Charleston obstetrician, through her professional midwives' association. Maura had thought that perhaps Bonnie's Dr. Urquehart might help her by supervising her own practice in Shuffletown; after all, he'd had experience in working with Bonnie, and for her own patients' hopefully rare needs for hospital care, Dr. Urquehart might prove ideal.

"Dr. Urquehart is coming to a party at my house Friday night," Bonnie had told her over the phone. "Just a group of medical professionals from the Charleston area. You should feel right at home."

Meeting Dr. Urquehart on a social basis appealed to her, and after her disastrous idea about having Xan Copeland examine her, she couldn't entertain any foolish notions about making herself a guinea pig again. Bonnie was so friendly that Maura had agreed to come to the party. It wasn't until afterward that she'd worried about what she'd gotten herself into.

It wasn't the kind of party she had expected, she thought as she stood indecisively in front of the house, which was located in a new suburb on the outskirts of town. She'd thought there would be a few serious-minded medical people sitting around a well-furnished living room in a gracious old Charleston home, talking quietly above soft flute music from a cassette deck. Instead here was a strobe-lit modern house fairly rocking on its foundations with music louder than any she'd ever heard, and a veritable stream of people flowing in and out the front door.

"Don't just stand here, you'll get trampled," shouted one of several rowdy young men who stampeded toward the door as Maura was trying to decide whether she should stay or go. All of a sudden that question was decided for her: two of the men on either side of her wrapped their arms around her waist and fairly lifted her off the ground as they swept her along with them into the smoky hallway of the house. "She who hesitates is lost," one of the men intoned with a wink and a leer before abandoning her for the kitchen, where it appeared there were drinks.

Hors d'oeuvres on the dining-room table in the room to the right languished neglected in lank beds of no-longer-crisp endive. People in the room on the left were dancing with wild abandon, and Maura stared fascinated as various parts of their bodies jiggled in frenzy.

"Want to dance?" The question was articulated behind her, and she whirled to recognize one of the fellows who had borne her into the house.

"I . .can't," she said, peering at him through the smoke. He looked woozy, as though he had already had too much to drink.

"Hah," he said. "That's pretty good. You can't?"

Maura nodded, sure it wasn't worth explaining. But she couldn't imagine herself in that crush of people, flinging her body around in such an obviously sexual way Those long-ago dances in St. Bridget's High School gym had been, well, prim.

"Why don't you just say you don't want to dance with me?" He was leaning toward her belligerently; his tone of voice made her uncomfortable and she recoiled sharply at the blast of his beery breath. She should have left, she thought despairingly, before she ever came inside.

Then, rescue. "Maura McNeill?"

She whirled to see a young brunette, petite and personable, looking up at her with interest. "Yes," Maura said, no longer worried. There was warmth and depth in the other woman's gray eyes.

"Bonnie Trenholm," said the brunette, holding out her hand. "Bert," she said to the young man, "DeeDee is looking for you. In the den."

"DeeDee," he bellowed, forging off down the hall, Maura forgotten. "Where are you, dear heart?"

"Ignore him," advised Bonnie. "He's an intern from the hospital. Gets drunk every weekend. I didn't invite him, but DeeDee did. She's a student nurse and has the most disgusting crush on him. Can't imagine why. But that's the way it is around hospitals, particularly hospitals attached to medical schools. You know all about that, I suppose."

Maura shook her head. Bonnie guided her up a nearby flight of stairs and sat down on the carpeted landing. She patted the stair beside her. "Sit down," she said, grinning up at Maura. "This looks like a fairly quiet place for the time being."

"I don't know much about...well, dating situations around hospitals," Maura confessed. She felt she could be frank with Bonnie; the other midwife seemed kind and understanding. "I—I came here right out of a convent. I took my nurse's training as a nun."

Bonnie stared for a moment. "Good heavens, and I invited you to this party? You must feel completely out of your element."

"That's for sure," said Maura fervently. "I really only came to meet Dr. Urquehart. I thought a social situation..." and then her voice died out uncertainly as she peered through the rungs in the stair railing at the writhing bodies in the room below. With the smoke and the flashing strobe lights, they looked like people out of one of those awful frightening paintings of Dante's Inferno.

"Don't worry," said Bonnie sympathetically. Her very sympathy made Maura trust her. "I'll corner

Alan Urquehart and tell him you want to talk with him privately. I won't tell him you're an ex-nun unless you want me to."

"No, don't tell him," said Maura quickly. "When they know I'm an ex-nun, people see me in a different light. I want to appear as—as normal as possible. And my being an ex-nun shouldn't enter into whether Dr. Urquehart wants to sponsor my practice or not."

Bonnie squeezed her arm. "Of course it shouldn't. Okay. Go wait on the patio on the wicker settee and I'll send him out. Then you can stay at the party or leave afterward, whichever you'd feel more comfortable doing."

"I think," said Maura slowly, "I'd better go. Life in the convent didn't prepare me for this sort of social situation. I have some growing up to do before I can handle it." She couldn't possibly explain her inner distress at the certain knowledge that she was ill-equipped for survival at a gathering like this.

Maura waited uneasily on the settee on the patio for Alan Urquehart, nervous about being approached by one of the many other men present and ill at ease about her interview with Dr. Urquehart. The wicker on the back of the settee cut uncomfortably into her upper arms; she edged slightly forward and folded her hands in her lap, rehearsing what she would say. She knew she'd have only a few moments to make Dr. Urquehart see the urgency of her situation and how much she needed him to provide the all-important medical backup for her practice. Dr. Urquehart was one of the best ob-gyn men in the Charleston area, and he was on the staff of the largest hospital in Charleston.

Finally, after what seemed like a long time, a middle-aged man came out of the house, closing the door quietly behind him. "Ms. McNeill?" he said, peering at her through glasses with lenses as thick as the bottoms of Coke bottles.

"Yes," she said, thinking that she needn't have worried so much. Alan Urquehart was a kindly, portly man who smiled at her reassuringly.

"Bonnie tells me you're planning to start a practice in midwifery," he said, sitting down beside her. Maura's qualms faded away, and suddenly it was easy to talk to Dr. Urquehart about her hopes and dreams for the people of Shuffletown.

"I know what I'm asking you to do is highly unusual," she said earnestly when she had finished her plea. "But I'll move my patients to Charleston only if their medical condition absolutely requires it."

"And how do you plan to transport when necessary?"

"In my van if time isn't a problem. By ambulance if it is."

Alan Urquehart regarded her consideringly, and as the moments ticked by, Maura realized that she was holding her breath in suspense. But then he nodded decisively. "I'll do it," he said, and Maura nearly fell out of the settee. She hadn't expected it to be so easy.

"I happen to believe that the women of Shuffletown are just as entitled to alternative birthing methods as anyone else, and you seem to be just the person to provide the thorough care that they need. I want to help you.'' He smiled warmly, and Maura could have thrown her arms around him. Instead they shook hands, and within a few minutes they had agreed on a loose working relationship that would provide the precious backup Maura needed. She thanked him profusely when they parted.

"You're going to be a good influence on the people of Shuffletown," he told her. "I'll help you in any way I can." His confidence in her made her feel wonderful.

Maura knew that Dr. Urquehart's respect for Bonnie Trenholm had given her a valuable boost, and so she sought Bonnie out in the crowded kitchen to tell her about Dr. Urquehart's wholehearted enthusiasm and to thank her for her recommendation.

"I'm glad it worked out," Bonnie said, clasping Maura's hand. "Let me know if there's anything else I can do to help."

Maura left Bonnie in the kitchen and pushed her way through the crush of people in the hall, trying to get outside. She stepped on a few toes, hardly caring, just longing for fresh air and freedom from this awful party.

And then she ran into him. Before she even lifted her eyes to his face, she recognized Xan by the distinctive whorled pattern of the dark hair on his chest above the unbuttoned top buttons of his pearl-gray knit shirt. She looked up and up to the cleft chin, to the less-than-perfect nose, to the dark-fringed green eyes, which were regarding her with amazement.

"Taking in a bit of the local social scene, I see," Xan said approvingly.

"I was just leaving," she managed to say, brushing past him.

"No, you weren't," he said, somehow wrapping his arms around her so that she could move no farther. "You were just about to dance with me."

"I can't dance," she said for the second time that night.

"Don't be ridiculous. Of course you can dance," he said, and to prove it he maneuvered her until her right hand was in his left and her left was on his shoulder, and his right arm around her waist tugged her insistently in the direction his feet were moving.

She stumbled. He righted her. He peered down at her, frowning slightly and sniffing her breath. "Had a little too much to drink?"

She gulped. "Nothing to drink. I don't drink. At least I don't think I do." She recognized the song on the cassette player as a slow ballad, one she'd heard often enough on the van's radio during the long, lonely drive from California. Some level of awareness sorted out the rhythm to this dance, and she tried to recall the one-two-three, one-two-three of her dancing-school days. There had been this kid named Danny Riley who had usually been her partner. He'd had freckles on his ears.

"What do you mean, you don't *think* you drink? Not even wine with dinner?" He was looking exasperated now, and no wonder. His toes were under her feet more often than not.

"Wine? Oh, I suppose so," she said distractedly. He swooped her into a vacant place in the middle of the crowd of dancers. She gave his shoulder a little push with her left hand; he was holding her much too tightly.

"What was that supposed to mean?" he asked.

She flushed in embarrassment. "You're—you're holding me too closely," she said.

"You could follow me better if I held you even closer," he said, firmly pulling her body toward him until her breasts tipped his chest. She pulled away, but he rested his cheek on her temple, where she could just barely feel the slightly rough texture of recently shaved skin.

"You dance very nicely," he said with a hint of insincerity. And then "Oops" as she delivered a heel chop to his instep.

"I told you I didn't dance," she pointed out.

"That's right," said an all-too-familiar voice behind them. They both looked to see Bert, the tipsy intern who had asked Maura to dance earlier. He looked threatening. "You wouldn't dance with me. Why are you dancing with him?" He jerked an intimidating thumb at Xan.

"Leave her alone, Bert," said Xan in a low tone. "The lady's my date."

"Your date? But how...? She came in with us." He looked befuddled.

"And she's leaving with me," said Xan peremptorily. The cassette player was trailing out the last lingering notes of the song. "Shall we go, Maura?" He eyed her meaningfully.

With Bert scowling at both of them, there was nothing she could do but hook her arm through Xan's and let him escort her off the floor, leaving an angry-looking Bert standing there looking as though he'd like to kill someone if only he could figure out who. A few seconds later, they heard him yelling, "DeeDee? DeeDee!" Maura pitied the unseen DeeDee, wherever she was.

Xan spirited her outside, and then, looking pleased with himself, said, "Where to? It appears that you're my date. There's a good jazz trio playing at the Piccadilly Pub. Want to try it?"

"Xan, thanks for rescuing me, but I can't go out with you." She stopped in front of her van and pulled her keys out of her purse, jingling them slightly out of nervousness.

"Why not? Why are you always putting me off? Anyway, if you didn't want to socialize, why did you come here?" He stared at her, perplexed.

She inhaled a deep breath. "I came here because Bonnie Trenholm put in a good word for me with her supervising OB, Alan Urquehart, and I wanted to ask him if he'd be my supervising physician."

"And?" Xan was glowering down at her, more intimidating than she'd ever seen him.

"And he will. End of story. End of evening." She turned and slipped the key into the locked door.

Xan raked an impatient hand through his hair. The curls stood up on his head, no longer styled into neat waves. "So you got your way after all," he said in carefully measured tones.

Maura paused before getting into the van. "Does

that surprise you?" she tossed at him challenging-
ly.

He considered this. Then the suggestion of a smile
touched his lips. "No, Maura, my dear, it does not.
You are a determined individual with stubborn ideas.
You wanted to get your way and you did. Congratula-
tions." His lip curled back, and it was not quite the
smile she thought it was at first. The glint in his eyes
cut through her.

Stubborn. Determined. Well, she had been referred
to in those terms before. His words echoed those of
the mother superior when she had demanded that
Maura discontinue her outreach practice in midwifery. Stubborn and determined were not words that
should apply to a nun. But they were not an unwelcome description now; in fact they only underscored
her dedication to the people of Shuffletown.

The smile that lit her features was brilliant and not
at all what he had expected. "Thank you," she said,
slamming the door after her.

"Wait a minute," he said tightly, wrenching the
door open again. "You got your way. And now I'm
going to get mine."

And then he pulled her down from the van seat,
made her tumble into his arms. "Maura McNeill," he
said, and again she could see twin moons reflected in
the mossy-green depths of his eyes as the warm flut-
ter of her name became his breath upon her lips. Her
lips parted in surprise as his face bent over hers, and
she gasped in shock. His mouth was open as it
touched her lips, sucking the breath out of her, pos-

sessing the very air she breathed, replacing it with his own. His lips sought the corners and crevices of hers, savored the fullnesses and the flavors, and her startled response was a sensation of weakness overshadowed by awareness. Surely and masterfully he angled her head into the proper position, swung his arm around her to cradle it, and the force of her heartbeat pumped unforeseen sensations through her in great hot waves.

Her hands touched him tentatively at first, searching for support as he bent her over his arm, but once they felt the warm surging strength of his muscles beneath the knit fabric of his shirt, she no longer seemed to be able to control their direction. Her fingers felt their way over his rippling biceps, lingered numbly for a moment on the hardness of his shoulders, slid deliberately to his neck, where they rested at the nape, barely tipping the short curly hair there.

His other arm, the one that wasn't supporting her head, circled her upper back, pressing her firmly against his body so that she could feel his well-defined pectoral muscles straining against her swelling breasts, now so sensitive that she could do nothing but arch against him, longing for him to release their tautness with his sure and knowing touch.

This shouldn't be happening, she told herself helplessly, and then his tongue found the opening it needed and invaded her with a forcefulness that left her no more time for that kind of thinking. A new kind of thinking took hold, a rationalizing sort of thought that fooled her into believing that somehow it was right to be doing this with Xan Copeland. It had to be right because it felt so good.

With consummate skill his tongue mimicked the sexual act, teaching her more in three minutes than she'd learned in her whole lifetime. Her mouth had opened to him and it was all delight, all pleasure to be swept away like this, to be so closely a part of him.

"You see," he murmured huskily against her throat when he had finally released her lips only to leave her gasping in his ear and longing for more. "This is good for both of us, Maura."

Xan's breath fairly sizzled on her skin, and she knew that if she allowed this to go on, the results could only be disastrous. She pushed him away, but only a little. He had pinned her so tightly against him that he would have to be the one to release her.

"It's all happening much too fast," she told him shakily.

"I don't think it's happening fast enough," he said wryly, and when she looked at him more sharply, she could see that he wore a look of dry amusement.

Oh, the things she could tell him if she would! Maybe their relationship wasn't moving fast enough by the standards of most people, but Maura felt completely out of sync. And one thing she knew was that she did not want to be a fast pickup at a wild party. She shook her head as if to clear the cobwebs from it, and her look of confusion and disorientation made Xan take a small step backward.

She avoided the peril of his eyes. "I want to go

home now," she said firmly, surprising herself at the resoluteness of her tone.

"Well, lady, if you insist. But you're really missing something." His eyes glittered with humor, and she was sure he didn't mean that what she would be missing was the party.

He didn't stop her when she climbed back into the high seat of the van and slammed the door. He didn't say a word as she started the engine. And as she rolled away from the curb, trying to pull the world back into focus despite the crazy pounding of her heart, he only raised his hand in a silent salute of farewell.

It seemed like a very long drive back to Teoway Island, but the time gave Maura a chance to think. And what she thought was that her body could betray her if she let it. Not that it was bad for her body to feel so good—she had left that idea behind forever. But she couldn't get involved with Xan Copeland— *wouldn't* get involved with Xan Copeland. Her time and her energy were needed elsewhere.

AFTER THE NIGHT of the party, Xan faded from Maura's life, if not from her thoughts. She tried not to think about him or his consummate skill at lovemaking; indeed, going ahead with her plans to become a practicing midwife dominated her life. Converting the farmhouse to the McNeill Birth Center became Maura's focus during the next few weeks.

"This will be my waiting room," Maura told an interested Kathleen, who had finally, with reservations, come to look, "and the former living room can func-

tion as an exercise and education room. And here"—
Maura indicated a sunroom—"I'll install a playroom
with toys for the young children accompanying their
parents." Two first-floor bedrooms would be trans-
formed into examining rooms. Outside, a sign that proclaimed McNEILL BIRTH CENTER swung from a branch of
one of the pecan trees.

Kathleen looked around at the sunny house. When
Maura had first told her about it, she hadn't been able
to imagine how an old farmhouse could become the
birth center Maura envisioned. She was happy to see
that it had a light, airy look about it. Maura had already painted the waiting room a soft shade of yellow;
plants would hang in front of the long windows of
what had formerly been a dining room.

"It's perfect," said Kathleen, her initial objections
to the old farmhouse overcome. "Just perfect. In fact
my friends on Teoway Island would love to come to
someplace like this for prenatal care."

"They're welcome, you know," said Maura. "The
NcNeill Birth Center will serve all women, not just
the ones from Shuffletown."

"Have the Shuffletown women shown any interest?"

"They're beginning to ask questions when they see
me around town. I've put signs up at the local Laun-
dromat and in the gas stations along the highway. My
telephone will be installed tomorrow, and I'm going
to move in here on Saturday."

Katheleen's face fell. "Really, Maura? I don't see
why you have to live here. Wouldn't you be more
comfortable staying with us on Teoway?"

"No, Kathleen," said Maura firmly. "We've been through all this before, and I haven't changed my mind. I'll be perfectly comfortable living upstairs."

"But it's so hot out here in the middle of these cotton fields, and it's so far from everything." Kathleen furrowed her forehead at her sister; why would Maura want to forsake the sumptuous comforts of Teoway for this isolated farmhouse?

"Thanks to the wonderful O'Malley Family Foundation, I can afford a couple of air conditioners and they're arriving"—she consulted a list on a clipboard—"tomorrow. So neither summer heat nor flies nor South Carolina's fabled gnats will stray this midwife from her chosen work. Now"—she smiled encouragingly at Kathleen, who still looked skeptical about Maura's insistence that she live here—"did someone mention lunch?"

And so they left in Kathleen's new silver-blue Thunderbird for a celebration lunch at the outdoor restaurant in the elegant Marketplace Mall on Teoway Island, and Maura looked around her at the carefree and luxurious surroundings that were beautiful but meant absolutely nothing. After the convent, life here seemed trivial and the people self-centered compared to the nuns among whom she had lived before. Maura knew beyond the shred of a doubt that she was doing the right thing for herself and for the people of Shuffletown by moving to her farmhouse.

"Has there been any reaction to your McNeill Birth Center from Xan Copeland?" Kathleen asked after the waitress had served them the house specialty, a concoction of scallops in white wine.

Maura shook her head. "Not a word," she said. "Nor do I expect any." Kathleen didn't know about Maura's disturbing encounter with Xan at Bonnie's party.

Kathleen nodded sagely. "It's probably just as well that you haven't heard from him," she said.

"Mmm" was all Maura said, and she bent her head so that her hair fell over the side of her face, effectively blocking Kathleen's view of her facial expression. She didn't want to tell Kathleen, but she would have given almost anything to know what Xan Copeland thought about the determined way she was going ahead with her birth center.

The day after her lunch with Kathleen, Maura was struggling to hang a pair of recalcitrant calico curtains in one of the examining rooms when she heard a timid knock at the door. It couldn't be the telephone installer because the telephone had already been put in, and it couldn't be the air-conditioning man because, unfortunately, he had called and postponed his delivery of the air conditioners until tomorrow. Suppressing irritation over the interruption, Maura tossed the curtains aside and clambered down the ladder, and when she arrived at the door she was surprised to find a little bit of a young woman with dark golden skin who stood peering anxiously through the screen door.

"Come in," Maura called, wiping her dusty hands on her smock. She half expected it to be someone who had read one of her signs and who was inquiring about prenatal care.

Her visitor broke into a big smile when she stepped

inside the door, reminding Maura of nothing so much as one of those yellow smiley-face stickers, and she said, "Ms. McNeill, Dr. Copeland sent me."

Maura couldn't have been more surprised, and evidently her amazement showed on her face. It seemed, however, that there was only one polite thing to do. "Well, I—well, okay. Do come in and sit down." She led her guest through the maze of boxes and cleaning supplies to the waiting room and pulled up a straight chair—for the moment the only furnishings in the waiting room were four straight chairs and a card table—and wondered who on earth this woman was and why Xan had sent her. Surely he couldn't be sending Maura patients!

"He said you need an assistant."

"I am looking for one," said Maura.

"My name is Golden Prescott, and I'm a nurse. I applied at the Quinby Hospital, but they didn't have an opening. Dr. Copeland said maybe you could use me."

"Where did you work before?"

"I was working at a hospital in Knoxville, but my mother got sick and I had to come back home to take care of her. Since she died, I'm all alone, and I need work." Golden spoke softly, and Maura found herself warming to her quiet voice and gentle manner.

"Are you interested in becoming a midwife? I need an assistant. I'll train you, but it's the kind of work you have to love."

"I worked in the maternity ward, so I know enough about mothers and babies to get by. Once I delivered a baby that came early, before the doctor got there. It—it made me feel special."

Maura asked her a few more relevant questions about her training and experience, but it was Golden's eyes, so eager and sincere, that really did the convincing. "Do you know anything about hanging curtains?" Maura asked finally.

Golden stared at her for a moment, and then she began to laugh. "Yes, Ms. McNeill, I do. Sounds like you need some help."

Maura stood up. "Come back here and hand these curtains up to me, then, while we talk about what I expect from my assistant. And call me Maura, please."

The terms of Golden's employment were settled as they straightened out the tangle of curtains, and Golden agreed to report to work the next day. They shook hands on the deal, and after Golden had left, Maura ironed another pair of curtains, ready to hang them upstairs. She couldn't believe that finding a promising assistant had been so easy.

And it probably wouldn't have been if Xan hadn't helped. She couldn't believe that he had cared enough to send Golden to her. Golden was a prize; she was exactly the kind of person with the right experience that Maura was looking for. Because she knew how Xan felt about her professional presence here, Maura realized that his sending Golden had been a generous gesture. Could there have been an ulterior motive in his sending Golden? Probably not. It seemed more as if he'd seen the opportunity to do both women a favor and had done it. She'd have to drop Xan a nice note and thank him.

Her eyes fell on the newly installed telephone. She hadn't even tried it out yet. Well, why not? She'd call Xan and thank him that way. It would be easier and less time-consuming than writing a note. She had to look up his office number in her new phone book. His receptionist answered, and when she gave her name, Maura was put on hold while the receptionist buzzed Xan.

He picked up the line immediately. "Maura?" he said, and he sounded as though he could hardly believe that it was she.

"Yes," she said. She didn't recall his voice having so much resonance; it was deeper than she remembered. She took a deep breath. "Thank you for sending Golden to me. She's perfect."

"I hoped she would be. It seemed to me that you might be right for each other. She needs a job."

"And I need her. I, um, appreciate your thoughtfulness." Suddenly she felt tongue-tied at the thought of Xan on the other end of the line.

"I wanted to do something for you." His voice was tight, as though he were suppressing emotion. Maura didn't know what to say, but suddenly there was a lump in her throat.

"Look, Maura, maybe we could have dinner together tonight," he said, surprising her.

Her thoughts in a turmoil, she looked around at the jumble of boxes. Her mind felt in as much a jumble as her surroundings at the very thought of seeing Xan again. Anyway, she didn't have time to see him. Supplies had to be unpacked, floors had to be swept if she was ever going to get this clinic in apple-pie order.

"Oh, Xan, I appreciate your doing something so nice for me. But I've got so much to do. I'm getting my clinic ready to open."

"I know," he said. "I've seen your signs. Can't you get away for dinner?"

"Well, I really must finish up here. I'm moving my things in on Saturday. And if we were to go out, I'd have to go back to Kathleen's and shower. I don't know, Xan. It's not a good time."

"Any time is a good time," he insisted. "How about if I come over and help you with what you have to do after I leave the office? Then you'll finish up early and we can play it by ear after that. If you don't feel like going out, I can toss a meal together at my place. Come on, Maura. How can you pass up an offer like that?"

She had to laugh at his coaxing. "I suppose I can't." She hesitated. She was tired of all the backbreaking work she'd been doing. She would enjoy being spirited away from it, forgetting everything for a while. Her heart lifted at the thought of seeing Xan again. Impulsively pushing aside all the reasons she shouldn't, she said, "If you really mean it, I'll be looking for you. Are you any good at hanging curtains?"

"We'll find out. I'll see you around five-thirty." He sounded jubilant, and Maura found herself smiling into the phone. When she hung up, she was still smiling. She couldn't believe how much she was looking forward to seeing him.

She ironed more curtains and draperies, so by the time Xan arrived, she had several pairs ready to hang. She was standing at the ironing board finishing up the last panel when she saw his Cadillac pull up in front.

Xan bounded up the porch steps and rapped on the door. She wasn't prepared; she had thought she would run a brush through her hair and splash cool water on her hot cheeks before he arrived. She lifted both hands to her face and pushed back the damp tendrils of hair that kept falling forward as she ironed. "Hi," she said through he screen door. "Come in."

He opened the door and looked around in consternation. "You're right—you do need some help," he said.

She smiled at him, pure radiance. He had forgotten that smile of hers, so brilliant and genuine. He hadn't, however, forgotten the shape of her or her unselfconscious sexuality, which had taken over his mind in the past few weeks so that he could hardly think about anything else. Her face was slightly flushed and shiny with perspiration from the heat of the iron. He thought she was beautiful.

"I'd like to hang these curtains before I leave," she told him. "They belong upstairs."

"No problem," he said. He threaded his way through the clutter of boxes and looked around. "Is this your waiting room?"

"Yes," she said. She hadn't expected him to be curious about her clinic. She'd thought he'd skirt around the subject. Although, with everything still such a mess, it was a difficult subject to ignore.

He walked across the hall to the former living room. It was a big, wide room with a polished hardwood floor. Bookshelves held various pamphlets that Maura would hand out to her patients, but there was no furniture because she would teach exercise and yoga classes there. When necessary for group meetings, she would set up folding chairs for her patients.

"What's this room?" he wanted to know.

"Education and exercise room," she told him, unplugging the iron.

He turned around, lifting his eyebrows. "Exercise? What kind of exercise?"

She hoped he wasn't going to get critical of her methods. She didn't want the evening to deteriorate into arguments about whose ideas about childbirth were right. She wouldn't have agreed to see him if she'd thought that was what was going to happen. "Exercise to help my patients deliver healthy babies," she said. "Will you carry the stepladder upstairs for me? I can manage the curtains."

He grinned at her. "Okay. Subject closed for the time being. Where's the ladder?"

She indicated the examining room and preceded him upstairs, feeling overly conscious of his eyes upon her legs. There were three bedrooms upstairs. One would be her sitting room, another her office, and the biggest her bedroom.

They hung the office curtains first. They were simple hopsacking panels with fringe trim on the edges and tiebacks. The sitting-room curtains were lightweight and airy and went up fast.

Xan held the ladder steady as she worked to get the bedroom curtains straight in a room made stuffy by unopened windows and no air conditioning. "Just one thing I'm worried about," she said, trying to fit the curtain rod into its bracket. "The morning sun is going to shine right in these windows. I'm afraid it'll be hot, and on the occasional mornings when I want to sleep late, it'll wake me up."

"Get light-blocking window shades," Xan suggested.

"Mmm," she said, finally locking the rod in place. "Good idea." She turned and smiled at Xan as she descended, and then a shadow of movement rippled in the corner of the room. Her eyes widened. "A mouse!" she yelped, and she was so startled that she jumped. She wasn't afraid of mice. It was just that she hadn't expected to see something alive and furry in just that place at that time.

Her sudden movement was enough to send her slightly off balance. For a precarious second she wobbled, and Xan's free arm went up to grasp her around the waist and steady her. Then her feet were both on the ground and Xan's arm was still on her waist, and she felt herself being drawn inexorably closer. It had been hot in the room before, but now it seemed hotter still: she felt the heat radiating from Xan's body and flowing through her body, and she went weak from the force of it.

"I'll buy you a mousetrap," he said, staring down at her.

"A cat," she replied, caught in the trap of his eyes. "I'd rather have a cat. For company."

"I like cats," he said, his voice trembling, and she knew that he wasn't talking about cats at all.

"Xan," she said, pushing him away, but it was too late for that. His face was dangerously close to hers, so close that she could see straight into his eyes, into the deep dark depths, so cool and inviting. Her heart pounded and she could feel her own pulse in her ears. The beat of it blotted out every other sound—the chattering of squirrels in the trees, the hum of a far-away tractor in a cotton field.

And then she lost track of parts of her—her arms and legs and toes and fingers, all of which seemed unimportant because she could feel only the parts of her body that were relevant to this particular experience. Her lips, now parted and unable to remove themselves from his space; her skin, tingling where his arm encircled her waist; and a deep throbbing center of which she had never been aware before.

His lips touched hers tentatively, and she could feel his warm breath upon her skin. She stopped breathing, stopped thinking, stopped wanting him to stop. Now she wanted this as much as he did, and her heart filled with gladness as he clasped her body close to his and proceeded to kiss her with a tenderness that made her feel cherished and wanted and loved.

Her arms found their way around him, pressing him closer so that she could feel the lean hardness of him, so that their bodies fit with a precision she could never have imagined even if she had tried. Compared with their passionate coming together on previous occasions, this kiss was thoughtful and caring and full of meaning. It was pleasant and not at all frightening in the way Xan's other lovemaking had been. Yet it made her aware of an empty place inside her, a place of which she had only vaguely been aware before now. *So this is what it's all about,* she thought, the words singing themselves through her head, and she willingly, without his forcing it, opened her lips to his so that she could feel even more.

It was hot in the room, but the heat only made their contact more intense. When finally he released her mouth, she moaned low in her throat, not even knowing that she did. He didn't let her go, only held her in his arms for a very long time so that she could hear the beating of his heart until gradually their breathing returned to normal and they reluctantly pulled apart.

Maura stared at him, her heart in her eyes, and he thought to himself that never before with any other woman had kissing seemed so perfect and so right. He raised his hand almost reverently and drew one finger across those marvelous, well-shaped lips, now slightly parted in a kind of startled wonder. "You look as though you've never been kissed before," he said softly, overwhelmed by the wholly emotional response he had stirred in her.

She lowered her eyelids in confusion. Quickly gathering herself together, she wondered if the kisses had been as important to him as they'd been to her.

What had he felt while she was practically swooning in his arms? What had he been thinking? Did he know what she had been thinking? No, he couldn't have.

She knew herself well enough to realize that something important had happened to her when he had kissed her, something crucial to her sense of self. In those moments, she had accepted herself for the first time as a desirable female—nothing earthshaking to the average woman, perhaps, but for someone of her convent background it was an admission of amazing possibilities. Never before had she accepted the thought of herself as anyone a man would want, or as an embodiment of feminine charms.

She had realized, at Kathleen's urging and with a lot of difficulty, that she'd have to look at men in a new way now. But never had anyone told her that she'd eventually learn to look at herself in a new way. So she was unprepared for this stunning moment of self-revelation.

"You're one of the most fascinating women I have ever met," Xan said, his voice a low murmur. "You are so natural and unassuming that I can almost forget that we hold opposite views on a very important matter."

Her eyes shot to his. "What is that supposed to mean?" she breathed.

"It means we'd better not get into any conversations about the manner in which women should give birth," he said, with a humorous quirk to his mouth. "But somehow I think we'll be able to find other things to discuss, don't you?"

"Oh, yes," she said glibly, amazed at her newfound ability to fence and hedge with a man clearly accustomed to lovemaking. "We'll find other things to discuss. Like dinner, for instance." Her sparkling eyes returned his humor with a new kind of assurance, and she knew with a blithe soaring of her self-confidence that she had replied in exactly the right way for this situation and this man. And then she turned and walked ahead of him out of the room and down the stairs, aware of his eyes upon her and happily feeling not at all self-conscious about this or anything else.

Chapter Seven

It was later that night, while she was dressing to go to Xan's villa for dinner, that Maura found herself telling a stupefied Kathleen about her growing relationship with Xan Copeland.

Kathleen, once the most popular girl at St. Bridget's High School, would seem to be the one person Maura could rely upon for advice and encouragement about relationships. Kathleen had always been utterly social, a smiler and a charmer who had pleased the nuns of St. Bridget's most of all by becoming an excellent student. No one was surprised when after high school she won a scholarship to a posh women's college in the East, least of all Kathleen. After a four-year whirl of dating all the most eligible men around, she'd wound up with Don, a real catch. So why wasn't she thrilled about Maura and Xan?

"You don't understand men," she told Maura flatly. "And tonight, with Xan Copeland, you're *not* going to the senior prom. This is a little more serious than that."

Maura's hairbrush stopped in midstroke and she met Kathleen's eyes in the mirror. "I didn't go to the senior prom," she reminded her sister, purposely taking the remark literally.

"Oh, I remember it well," said Kathleen with a tinge of irony. "You didn't want to go with either of the boys who asked you, so you stayed home and watched a rerun of *The Sound of Music* on television. That seemed sort of silly to me at the time."

Maura set her hairbrush on the marble vanity with a clatter and turned to face Kathleen. Then, shrugging her shoulders and smiling slightly, she went to sit down on the bed next to her. "Kath, it was anything but silly. That night when I watched the mother superior in the movie singing that song about climbing every mountain and finding a dream that will last the rest of your life, the magic of the song and the movie made me want to find my own dream."

"And so you tried," said Kathleen, moved by the fleeting sadness of Maura's expression.

Maura stood up. "I tried," she said, nodding. "But the dream didn't last." She turned her back and walked to the closet, choosing without much thought a zippered jumpsuit of topaz-colored raw silk. Remembering that long-ago night, she suddenly felt very discouraged. The night of that prom had been a turning point in her life, but, as often is the case, things had not turned out according to plan.

The young Maura's thoughts had been permeated by her mother's idealism, and by the time she was in her senior year in high school she'd been searching

for a dream. The night of the prom, while her class-
mates had been dancing their youth away, she had
watched the movie and then had vowed, "I *will* tackle
the world." At eighteen, anything and everything had
seemed possible.

The good sisters of the nursing order to which
Maura was referred by the principal of St. Bridget's
were delighted to welcome this starry-eyed idealist
into their convent. She had donned the pristine white
habit of the order and had solemnly promised to give
up possession of worldly goods, to obey her superiors
in the order, and to remain unmarried. She'd proudly
worn a band of white gold on the third finger of her
left hand, signifying her status as a bride of Christ.

Sister Maura had eagerly trained to be a nurse. It
was a chance to serve people in a special way, a vocation for which few were chosen. She accommodated
to the rules of her order; at the impressionable age of
eighteen, that wasn't hard to do. Nursing was hard
work, and it brought her down to earth soon enough.
But her ideals still flew like a kite in the wind, ready to
be reeled in at the right time.

"Ten years in the convent," Maura said, almost as
if to herself. "And then to leave it. I can't shake the
idea that I've thrown away the chance to serve people
in a really special way."

"Nonsense," scoffed Kathleen briskly. "You'll
change enough lives in Shuffletown with these new
midwifery ideas of yours. Anyway, you're just having
an attack of the guilts for leaving the order."

"Mmm," said Maura. "You know, Kathleen, I still

can't really talk about it. Not even to you." Unconsciously her thumb felt for the white-gold band on her ring finger. She still couldn't get used to its absence.

How hard it had been to leave the people she had served as a midwife when she belonged to the order! But she couldn't have stayed, not when her dream was in conflict with the wishes of her superiors. She would never forget the austere, tight-lipped gaze of the mother superior on the day she had handed Maura her ultimatum. To think about it now, so many months later, still made Maura want to weep for the loss of the ideals that had been so important to her.

It had happened so gradually, Maura's rebellion against the rules. Leaving the convent to conduct home births, she had discovered that she liked being the person in charge at birthings, liked being the one to whom everyone looked for guidance and advice. As time went on, it had become increasingly difficult for her, when she returned to the convent each time, to switch back into the obedient Sister Maura she was expected to be. In the end, her vow of obedience had been the one vow Maura couldn't countenance.

And so, finding the stance of the convent hierarchy on this particular vow untenable, she had fled, carrying the shreds of her dream with her, hoping to find a place where she could mend the tatters into some sort of whole again, where she could be the kind of midwife she wanted to be. And she had found Shuffletown, where she was needed.

But Maura wasn't going to indulge in feeling sorry for herself. The past was over, and her future looked bright. She fluffed her hair out over the collar of the jumpsuit. She had begun a new life, a good life, and tonight she was seeing Xan Copeland.

Kathleen, watching her sister's face, knew she had to make Maura see how concerned she was about her adjustment to the real world. She chose her words carefully. "Maura, there are a few things you should know about Xan Copeland," she said earnestly. "The first is that you shouldn't get involved with him. I know he's extremely good-looking and—"

"Why shouldn't I get involved with him?" Maura was openly curious.

Her sister's very innocence stiffened Kathleen's resolve. She spoke swiftly. "Xan sees many women. They lose their hearts to him, but he never takes any of it seriously. And then he's out of their lives, leaving them sadder but hopefully wiser. Maura, I don't want to see you hurt."

"I honestly don't see how that can affect me," said Maura patiently. "I'm not going to fall head over heels in love with him. You know me better than that." She tried to smile encouragingly at Kathleen.

Since this approach didn't seem to be working, Kathleen decided to try another tack. "I thought you and Xan were adversaries," she said. "I mean, didn't you tell me that you're at odds about childbirth methods?"

"Adversaries?" said Maura. "That's a very strong word. Anyway, whatever hostilities over childbirth methods might have existed between us have been defused." She gave her hair a final fillip with her brush and decided to explain. "Xan knows that Dr. Urquehart has agreed to be my medical sponsor, so that takes the pressure off him. And as sort of a peace offering, I think, Xan did the nicest thing for me today," she said. "He sent a woman—Golden Prescott—to my clinic to see me. She's going to be my assistant. And he was kind enough to come over to help me hang curtains upstairs after he left the office. I don't know that Xan and I are ever going to agree about birthing methods, but we've reached a sort of a truce. And I do like him, Kathleen."

Kathleen's troubled gaze took in her sister's bright happiness, and she realized that no matter what she said, Maura would not understand. Maura had lived apart from the real world for too long, a world where changing mores and life-styles had made the old ways of dealing with relationships obsolete.

"Maura, men expect more now. It's not like it was in high school. I'm afraid he'll want more than you can give." Kathleen raised her hands helplessly, because Maura was shaking her head. Clearly Maura wasn't going to believe Kathleen's theory that Xan had cold-bloodedly sat down and thought out exactly what would put him in a good light as far as Maura was concerned, and then had done it. He had sent Golden to her, and Maura, in her rush of gratitude over the gesture, had softened toward him.

Unaware of the cynical thoughts running through her sister's head, Maura put a reassuring hand on Kathleen's arm. "Don't worry, I can handle Xan. Really." Even while she was trying to communicate her confidence, Maura saw that she had failed abysmally. Kathleen looked more worried than ever, wishing she'd been more explicit about her opinion of Xan's intentions but knowing it wouldn't have done one bit of good. Maura was accustomed to seeking out the best in people, and she would do the same with Xan Copeland. All Kathleen could do was hope that her suspicions about Xan weren't true.

In the meantime, Maura tossed her comb, brush and wallet into another purse and burrowed into the depths of the vanity cabinet to find a small purse-size packet of tissues, humming to herself in a way that she hoped would set Kathleen's mind at rest.

As Maura waited for Xan to arrive, Kathleen hovered over her almost like an anxious mother seeing her young teenager off on her first date. Maura wished Kathleen would stop following her around the house, all but clucking like a mother hen, and most of all she wished Xan would hurry up. Finally she even wished that she had told Xan she would walk to his villa, just to spare herself from Kathleen's cloying overprotectiveness.

And then suddenly he was there, striding toward the door in his casual pale-blue pants, trim and fitted across his flat abdomen, accentuating the long muscles of his thighs, and with an open-throated white shirt to contrast boldly with his tan, and Maura had to catch her breath at the beauty of him. In that instant, confronted by the reality of Xan, not just the idea of him, Maura understood a glimmering of what Kathleen had been trying to tell her. She realized all at once how utterly protected she had always been, first by her home life, then by the convent. Man-woman relationships, up until now, had been somebody else's fantasy.

It was a lot to flash through her mind in those few moments as Xan strode between his car and the front door, but she shot Kathleen a mute look, and in that look Kathleen saw at least some part of the understanding that she had tried to impart. She fervently hoped it would be enough.

"MMM, YOU LOOK WONDERFUL," Xan told Maura as he held the door of his gleaming Cadillac open for her, and he grazed her cheek with his lips as she brushed past him, causing Maura to wonder if it was all right to allow such liberties, or if such a light brushing of lips to cheek could even be considered a liberty.

It was only a short drive to his villa. The villa faced the ocean, a two-story structure of cedar siding silvered like a piece of driftwood washed up from the sea. It was a light, open, airy place, with windows angled toward the ocean to take advantage of the view, and with sweeping decks cooled by the salty breeze from the sea. The deck outside the living room overlooked the dunes, and this was where Xan grilled their steaks.

"Sit down here beside me while I keep an eye on our dinner," he suggested, pulling a pair of canvas deck chairs together. He went back into the house, whistling, and emerged with a wine bottle and two cut-crystal glasses.

"Wine with dinner is all right with you, I presume?" he asked, slanting her a questioning look. She nodded, figuring that a bit of wine with a meal wasn't so very different from the wine at communion. He popped the cork and poured with practiced aplomb. Maura found herself holding her stemmed wineglass between thumb and forefinger and swirling its ruby contents as though she drank wine with dinner every evening.

And then he lit candles on a nearby table, and they sat and ate their dinner with the song of the sea for background music. She felt herself relaxing and unwinding, perhaps from the wine, perhaps from the delightful ambience of candle glow on weathered wood and the tang of the sea air, and a handsome male face wearing an expression that told her she was beautiful and fascinating.

Was she beautiful? No, Kathleen was the pretty one. Was she fascinating? She didn't see how she could be. She was just herself. That was all she knew how to be.

"So tell me, how does a registered nurse learn midwifery?" he said when they had eaten and were watching the candles build up odd windswept runnels of wax as they burned low in their brass holders.

"I thought we weren't going to talk about things like that," she objected. It was too pleasant an evening to ruin with arguments.

"Can't we talk about them if we don't snap at each other? I'm on my best behavior tonight," and he smiled at her appealingly, the cleft in his chin deepening in the flickering candlelight.

"I was working as a nurse in California," she said, remembering. She left out the part about being a nun; she knew she couldn't talk about it without telling him about leaving the convent, which was a subject too painful to explore.

"I worked in the hospital delivery room, and I often admired the courage of women who were about to give birth. They drew on a strength they never knew they had, most of them, and there was something noble about them in my eyes. I found myself forging a bond with those women, and yet when it was time for the baby to be born, the responsibility was shifted to someone else—the attending doctor." She stopped, thinking that perhaps she had gone too far.

But an understanding light flared in his eyes, and he said, "Go on."

"For a long time I wanted to expand on my relationships with these new mothers, but I didn't know how. Then a woman who was a midwife came into the delivery room as a coach for a mother who had been going to have a home birth but had had to come to the hospital at the last minute because of a complication. And that's when I knew that it wasn't enough just to be the nurse in the delivery room anymore. I wanted to be a midwife. And so I did become a midwife, and I've never been sorry."

"And then you decided to start your own practice?"

Maura nodded. There had been more to it than that, with her lobbying within the convent to institute an outreach program whereby her patients could give birth in the comfort and privacy of their homes, and then the capitulation of the powers that be in the convent and their subsequent delight when Maura's outreach program proved to be a huge success. But she didn't want to go into all that now. After all the success, her outreach practice in midwifery had ultimately culminated in failure. Unfortunately, the failure dominated her thoughts whenever she allowed herself to think about it.

"It seems to me," Xan said, looking thoughtful, "that you might have done better to stay in California, where midwives are more accepted."

She stiffened. She dropped her eyes so that her straight lashes cast spiked shadows on her high cheekbones. If she wanted to tell him the whole story, this was the perfect time. But she couldn't.

"I—I couldn't stay there, Xan," she said painfully.

He knitted his brows. He had said the wrong thing; that was clear. He gave her time to elaborate, but she seemed to be undergoing some kind of mental struggle, and then the light dawned. She had no doubt left California because of a broken love affair. Why else would her face have undergone such a transformation; she looked as miserable as he had ever seen her, her whole expression twisted with inner pain. He wanted to comfort her, wanted her to be able to talk to him.

"If you'd like to talk about it, it's all right," he said gently. If the table hadn't been between them, he would have gathered her into his arms and let her pour her heart out to him. Instead, he reached across the table and covered her hand with his.

The action seemed to distract her. "Not right now," she said quickly, trying to cover up her lapse of control. It wasn't that he lacked caring or understanding; it was just that her leaving of the convent was so personal, so infinitely profound in its effect on her life.

He thought he saw the dampness of tears in her eyes before she blinked them away, and he wanted to kill the bastard, whoever he was. In a surge of protectiveness, he determined to know the whole story someday, and then he would hold her close and reassure her that she was beautiful and desirable and loved, no matter what the guy had done to her.

"It's all right," he said thickly. "I'm glad you're here, not in California."

Maura swallowed and lifted her eyes to him, surprised at the solicitude she saw there. Why, it really did matter to him that she had been through this trouble, even though he didn't know what it was! She had not expected this empathy from Xan Copeland. But it warmed her heart to him in a way that nothing else could have.

She turned her palm up and squeezed his hand in a gesture that meant more to him than a hundred superficial confidences, than a thousand whispered love words. He was touched deep inside by her silence, which because of the interplay of their hands was more eloquent than words.

"Let's go for a walk on the beach," he said quietly. "Sometimes I see deer running along the shore. It's a sight that I'd like to share with you."

The moon cast a shimmering silver path on the ocean as they walked along the hard-packed sand past neighboring villas strung along the beach, each lit from within, like a string of lanterns at the edge of the sea. "Last time we walked on the beach," said Maura, "we talked about me. What about your childhood?"

Xan's hand captured hers, his fingers lacing through her fingers as they walked. "I was a lonely little boy. My parents died in a freak ski-lift accident when I was a baby, so I had only Aunt Lucy—my great-aunt, really. We lived in Aunt Lucy's big old house on Broad Street in the historic section of Charleston."

"Kathleen took me on a tour of the historic section when I first arrived here. Those gracious old homes are beautiful. I can't believe you actually were fortunate enough to live in one!" Pictures of a young Xan sprang into mind: Xan sliding down great swooping curved banisters; Xan peering over pierced brick walls through loops of lavender wisteria blossoms; Xan barefoot and swinging on heavy wrought-iron gates.

Xan grimaced. Clearly his mental pictures of his childhood were not the same as Maura's. "We were genteel, but not wealthy. The windows were draped in musty worn velvet that crumbled into dust if I ran my fingers along its nap, and Aunt Lucy served our meals on an assortment of sterling-silver pieces that had to be polished and polished to the point of utter boredom."

"I take it that polishing the silver was your job?"

"I'm afraid so. The meals we ate off that family silver were inelegant in the extreme. For a long time I thought everyone ate hot dogs off ornate silver salvers and ladled watery soup from heavy silver tureens. Aunt Lucy died in my last year of medical school, leaving an assortment of debts that took me years to pay off." He shook his head. "I always planned to start an ob-gyn practice in Shuffletown. When I found out I had to repay all the money she'd borrowed to keep our family home from falling apart, I almost had to give up on the idea."

"You could have made more money practicing obstetrics somewhere else," Maura pointed out.

Xan nodded. "I was tops in my class, and I was offered jobs with established medical practices in Atlanta, New York, and various cities east and west. I turned them all down. I was in a financial bind for a long time, but I paid off all Aunt Lucy's creditors."

"Why didn't you go to work for someone else for a little while? Until you paid off the money? You probably could have paid those debts a lot faster, and then you would have been free to start your practice in Shuffletown." Maura looked up at him. His chin was firm, and there was a determined spark in his eyes.

"That's what my fiancée said," he said.

"Your fiancée?" The word was difficult to say.

"Well, she was my fiancée at the time. She couldn't bear the idea of living quite that frugally, so when I told her I was going to open my practice in Shuffletown, she decamped."

"Oh. I'm sorry." It was all Maura could think of to say.

"Don't be. It was the best thing for both of us, I'm

sure. She eventually married a very wealthy man, and they have three well-behaved children, four status-symbol cars, and six homes, one to suit her every whim. For her, it's a far cry from Shuffletown. And I—well, there's never really been room for a woman in my life since then. I'm married to my practice, I suppose."

"Why is your practice so important to you?" She looked up at him curiously.

"The Shuffletown people need me. It's as simple as that. Some of them can't pay me; some of them pay me in food that they grow themselves or things that they make. I couldn't have faced myself every morning if all I had to think about was how much money I was going to rake in that day. To me, medicine isn't making money, although I'm doing well now. Medicine is for helping people."

"Oh, Xan, that's exactly how I feel! If only..." but her sentence died before she could utter it. She had been about to say, "If only we could work together." But with their different ideas about childbirth methods, that was impossible.

Instead, she asked him more about his childhood. He had spoken of his boyhood loneliness many times before, to many different women, but this time he felt like cutting the story short. He had always been well aware that his orphaned state made him the object of much sympathy, a sympathy that always worked well in his favor. By talking about it now, he knew that Maura, as kind and nurturing as she was, would be overinfluenced by it. And he wanted her to care for him on his own merits, not because of some overblown story of his life that he had used too many times for its emotional effect. The old games and gimmicks didn't work with her. He wasn't sure if this was good or bad.

As Xan spoke, Maura was once more very much aware of her attraction to him. She found herself wanting to feel his arms around her again; her skin prickled with the electricity of being near him. With embarrassment, she remembered the naïveté of her earlier assurances to Kathleen.

But how, she wondered in sheer desperation, was she supposed to learn all the things that most other women learned by osmosis and by living day by day? Her contemporaries were either married or single, many of them divorced, veterans of all kinds of love affairs, from the casual one-night stand to the liaison with a married man to the long-term commitment. Where did Maura fit into this complicated world? How was she going to catch up?

She hadn't thought she would be confronted with this issue so early. She had planned to sidestep all of it as long as she could. What she hadn't counted on was the entry of a handsome eligible man into her life.

Just then Xan stopped walking, and his hand slipped from hers and slid around her shoulders, effectively halting her, too. "Look," he said, pointing with his free hand toward the beach ahead of them.

A solitary white-tailed deer stood at the edge of the sea, its head raised, almost a shadow against the moonlit sand. It was utterly beautiful in its innocence as it stood there, with the path of the moon spread out over the gently undulating water. Maura had to catch her breath at the sight. As they watched, the deer wheeled and trotted along the shore, then turned and walked gracefully toward the dunes, where it disappeared, after one last look toward them, into a thicket of wax myrtle.

Xan said, "Often when I come home late at night, I'll sit out on one of the decks, especially if I've been officiating at a difficult delivery. It's so peaceful and quiet, and drinking in the beauty of this place helps me to relax. Deer slip in and out of the dunes like moonlit phantoms. Sometimes in the morning I'll find their footprints leading right up to my house."

They were approaching his house now. His arm remained around her shoulders, comfortable there. "What an enchanting house it is," said Maura, admiring the set of it from where they walked.

"I designed it myself." he said. "I wanted something that would display the sea to its best advantage, a place where I could include the natural beauty of this island as part of the decor."

Maura thought about the furnishings she'd seen inside. There was old mixed with new, grasscloth on the walls, dark wood tones interspersed with light. "You've succeeded," she told him. "It suits you."

They mounted the stairs to the wooden deck, and Xan slid open the sliding glass door for her. She entered, not really knowing what was expected of her. Xan probably entertained women here all the time—women who knew much more than she did about talking to a man. She wondered what those other women were like. Sophisticated, probably, wearing stylish clothes, not hand-me-downs from a sister. Trailing expensive fragrances as they walked, such as Chanel No. 5 or—well, she didn't know the names of any other expensive perfumes. She didn't even own any cologne.

Waiting for some clue from him, watching him covertly as he slid the glass door closed behind them, she wandered awkwardly to the lighted curio cabinet, its open shelves displaying unusually crafted pottery jugs. "What are these?" she asked, picking one up and turning it to observe it better. It felt cool and smooth against her hands.

The jug she held was a small stoneware vessel not much larger than a coffee mug and modeled with a face on the side opposite the handle.

"It's a face vessel. I collect Afro-American art of the type made by South Carolina slaves. Do you like it?" Xan had moved close behind her.

"Yes," she said. She liked the drollness of the face vessel, an expression of the artist's sense of humor. She probably would never have thought of this simple pottery as art, although of course it was. She didn't really understand most art. But this, a piece she could put her hands on, she did understand.

"Let me show you some more of the things I've collected," Xan said, replacing the jug carefully on its shelf. He took her hand and led her up a flight of stairs to a landing where overhead spotlights shone on a quilt that in colorfully appliquéd blocks told the story of slave life. "You see, here are a man and woman jumping over a broom," Xan said, pointing to one square. "That's how slaves used to get married. In the days when slaves were often ignored by the church, jumping over a broom was a tradition left over from Africa and the only ceremony many of them had." He pointed to another square. "Here's a cotton field, and the workers with their long sacks are picking cotton. This is a very old quilt, made by a slave in 1859."

Up the next flight of stairs, a collection of interesting baskets hung on the wall. Maura followed Xan as he led the way. "These are baskets woven by the women in Shuffletown. They sell them to tourists in Charleston, but I received them as a fee for delivering babies; the parents were too poor to pay me, but I was happy to get these instead of money."

The baskets were ingenious coils of pliable grass. "The workmanship is beautiful," said Maura, reaching out to trace her fingers along the spiraling fiber. It felt stiff to the touch.

"I'm glad you like it. You're likely to be paid in such things when you start your practice."

"I'll welcome anything anyone wants to give me in lieu of money," she said, thankful for the O'Malley Family Foundation grant that enabled her to say this. "It's not easy to furnish a place to live from scratch. And," she went on, hoping to make light of it, "scratch isn't comfortable to sit on."

He looked down at her, puzzled. "Don't you have furniture? Left over from California?"

"No," she said rather abruptly, and she eased herself out from under his arm and walked farther down the hall to the place where another quilt, this one a faded red-and-pink patchwork design, hung on the wall, also spotlighted by an eyeball light recessed in the ceiling.

"You'll have to buy some furniture, then," he said. "What kind of furniture do you like?"

She massaged her elbows, thinking of the ultramodern, all-too-clean lines of the furniture that Kathleen and most of her friends preferred. As a nun, she'd always looked at items in terms of their usefulness. Now, through Xan's eyes, she began to understand about the pleasurable possibilities of things she had taken for granted—furniture, art. There was a whole world of taste out there, just waiting for her to discover it. The thought tantalized her.

"I guess in furniture I'd like something with a little bit of character," she said thoughtfully. "Antiques, perhaps." Antiques would fit in well with the atmosphere of her farmhouse. And the patina of years on someone's discarded but once-loved furniture would give Maura herself a sense of ongoing history, of roots. She'd felt rootless ever since she'd cut herself off from the convent.

"Then you'll have to let me go shopping with you. I know some of the best places. Not the tourist traps in the downtown historic area, where they'll charge you an arm and a leg, but tiny shops where the markup isn't so high."

"I'd like that," she said. She looked at him curiously. "I'm surprised that you know about antiques."

"I learned from Aunt Lucy. Most of her things had to be sold to pay bills, but I managed to save a few of the pieces I liked. Look at this," and he took her hand again and drew her into what turned out to be a bedroom.

His bedroom, she thought nervously. She'd never been in a man's bedroom before. This was a particularly handsome one, dimly lighted by a lamp on the serpentine-front dresser and decorated in restful shades of green with peach accents. A huge four-poster bed covered with a white spread crocheted in a popcorn pattern dominated the room. Narrow wooden blinds, slanted to afford a view of the beach, masked the tall window.

"The bed is magnificent," she said, taking it in. Its mattress was so high off the floor that it had to be reached by three portable steps that had clearly been made just for climbing into this particular bed. The stair treads were covered with finely worked needlepoint pads, each bearing the Copeland family crest.

"It's called a rice bed," Xan told her. "See the rice plants carved into each of the four bedposts? It was in use on the Copeland rice plantation outside Charleston back in the 1700s."

Just looking at the bed made Maura nervous about Xan's designs on her. She turned away quickly toward the corner of the room, focusing on a painting on the wall. It was a pen-and-ink drawing of a Charleston street scene. It made her think that she'd need pictures, too, for her living quarters. She hadn't thought about furnishings for her farmhouse nearly enough, but she'd have to if she was going to make the house a real home. Suddenly, having a real home of her own, her very own place in the world, seemed urgently important.

"What is it like, living alone?" she asked, unaware of the poignancy of her question.

Xan's eyes shot toward hers and softened. "Lonely, sometimes," he admitted. He moved closer to her, his front to her back, blocking her exit from the corner. Her hair tumbled across her shoulders, wine-dark in the soft light from the lamp. Her hips in the snug jumpsuit swelled outward from the supple curve of her waist, and he ached to slide his hands around that waist and slowly smooth them downward.

"I'll have to get used to it, I suppose," she said, and then she couldn't speak anymore because she felt his intention and her body was responding despite her willing it to go on talking as before.

His hand beneath her hair was not at all unexpected. "Maura," he said, his voice deep in his throat, his breath caressing her abundant fall of hair, "I can't go on being near you without having something more."

She closed her eyes against the wave of warmth that swept upward from the region of her stomach, all thoughts of decorating her home swept aside. She was swirling in great sweeping circles, circles that encompassed her past, her present and her future, around and around, confusing her.

Who was she? Was she that Maura who had entered the convent at eighteen, sure of herself and her dreams? Or was she that Maura who had left California and the convent, her dreams shattered, bravely trying to pick up the pieces and go on with her life? Or was she the Maura who stood here, immobilized by one touch from Xan Copeland?

Before she met Xan, she had never felt lust. She had never felt love. She had no way of differentiating between the two emotions, no past experiences to set guidelines or limits. Despair at her own ignorance wrenched her heart: she felt like an utter fool.

In the meantime, Xan had narrowed the space between them. His fingers crept slowly down the sides of her neck, paused at the hollow of her throat to tarry over her throbbing pulse, moved surely to capture her shoulders in his strong grasp. Her head tipped backward of its own accord, her eyelids growing heavier and heavier until they closed. She inhaled deeply, his deep musky scent filling her nostrils and lingering seductively at the back of her throat.

"Sometimes," he said softly into her ear, his words no more than a warm breath, "it's terrible living alone. I don't like waking up alone, Maura."

Her head now rested against his shoulder, and she quickened to the strength of his muscles beneath the skin. And his arms were wrapping her close, his hands finding their way to her breasts, where they stroked gently, reverently, tantalizing her breasts so that they swelled and hardened temptingly at his touch. She arched backward into the feeling, so exquisite and pleasureful and threatening to exorcise all propriety.

"I love touching you," he whispered close to her ear. "You're so solid. All woman, but very vulnerable. Oh, Maura, be my woman." It was a heartfelt plea. He sensed her struggle for control, a struggle that was losing its fight for space amid her confused emotions. "Don't fight it," he urged. "Let me. Just...let me."

Languidly she submitted to the ease of it. It was so pleasant to flow along with him, swept into a tide of passion and loving that offered sweet oblivion to everything else. He rained kisses upon her arched throat, wet kisses that trailed exquisitely to the planes of her face, the angle of her jaw. She heedlessly sought his lips with hers, turning her face to his in mute offering, and, still behind her, he cupped the exposed curve of her cheek so that her lips might not escape while he drank his fill urgently.

She felt his passion straining against her, only half aware now of anything else but Xan. She revolved slowly within the circle of his arms until she faced him, staring at him unblinkingly, her eyes moist with longing.

Hands pressing her hips to him, he bent his head to kiss her perfect mouth, drifting his lips downward to the open throat of her jumpsuit, and Maura understood now for the first time her power as a woman. There was something heady about that power; she touched her lips to his dark hair and drew its scent into her nostrils, exhilarating in all her womanly power and in him.

It could have gone on, could have ended with the

two of them tossed among the billowed covers of that great high ancestral bed. It could have, but it didn't because of the zipper.

It was the sound of the zipper that brought her to her senses, that made her aware again of things beyond herself. The rasp of the slide over the teeth and the parting of the front of her jumpsuit, exposing one generously rounded breast to the coolness of the air, made her think. And what she thought was that she had been swept off her feet by an experienced practitioner of the art of seduction: she, who knew nothing of such things; she, whose convent background precluded the usual man-woman relationships; she, who was about to make a fool of herself and expose her very innocence. For she was innocent and untouched by any man—and she was afraid she wouldn't know how to make love to Xan Copeland.

She twisted away, at the same time conscious of a gut feeling that she should have gone through with it in spite of everything. For suddenly and unmistakably she knew that she had been made for giving to a man, for blending with him in that special way that had been denied to her until now. The knowledge shook her to the foundations of her soul. In all her soul-searching and self-examination, in all her intimate knowledge of herself, she had never realized that this forceful yearning, this passionate longing, was part of her makeup.

His hands remained on her shoulders, holding her so that she could not escape. His grip bit into her, and when he saw the pain he was causing her, he eased his grasp. "Maura, what's wrong?" he asked. He couldn't understand why she had pulled away. She was ripe for the taking, that was obvious from the look of her heavy eyelids, from the passion flaming in the depths of her eyes, from the flare of her nostrils and the parting of her lips.

"Xan, I can't," she breathed, and in a blaze of anguish he feared that she was thinking of the other man, the one she'd left behind in California.

He dropped his hands, and then with a determination that rose up inside him with an intensity of passion and longing, he crushed her to him, smothering her brief cry against his broad shoulder. "You can," he said fiercely, "and you will. If it's time you need, you can have time. I have lots of time. But make no mistake—I want to make love to you." He spoke raggedly, and then he shifted his weight backward, pressing her close with the arm around her waist but gripping her face in his other strong hand, gazing into her eyes with an expression so taut that she tried to shrink away from him but only succeeded in making him increase the pressure of his fingers on her jaw.

Her throat muscles were tight and aching with the strain of it, but she managed to say, "You don't understand, Xan, please." Doubt and confusion chased each other through her brain, making her wonder if she was doing the right thing.

"I understand more than you think I do," he said. "I didn't, however, figure you for a tease." He released her then, so suddenly that she almost fell when deprived of his support.

"I'm not a tease," she said indignantly. "There are other considerations, Xan. I—I need your patience," and here her voice dropped to no more than a whisper. But her look was so direct that Xan knew with a pang of instant comprehension that she was undergoing an inward struggle of the first magnitude. The other man, then—she was thinking of him.

Xan backed off, defeated. But he didn't intend to stay defeated. "I thought about it a long time before I asked you to come here for dinner," he said with deliberate frankness. "I didn't know if you'd accept the invitation or not."

"Well, now you know," she said, and then wished she hadn't said it.

He nodded, studying her. "I know only as much as you'll tell me," he said, waiting. It was an invitation, bald in its curiosity.

Maura didn't speak. She had been a fool to let things reach this point. Xan was a man who deserved better. He deserved an explanation, but she wasn't capable of giving it. If she had misled him, then she was sorry. She shook her head dumbly, unable to reply.

"Just for the record," he said dryly, "I don't make a pass at every woman who stays for dinner."

"Only the ones you lure into the bedroom?" she said, and then instantly regretted her uncharacteristic foray into the refuge of sarcasm.

"I don't usually have to lure them into my bedroom," he said darkly. "Nor do I use my collection of Afro-American art to get them there. You were interested—the first person who has ever shown any real interest, I might add. Anyway, there are other more exciting places to accomplish what we almost accomplished. Or didn't you know that?''

She clutched the two sides of the jumpsuit together, unsuccessfully trying to conceal her naked breasts from his eyes. She shook her head in confusion. Other more exciting places... her unaccustomed stab at sarcasm that felt all wrong as soon as the words had fallen from her mouth... she'd better get out of here before things took a turn for the worse.

When she moved to brush past him, Xan's finger on her cheek restrained her as it caressed the softness of her skin with a tenderness that told her he wasn't angry. A rush of relief overwhelmed her, and then his lips kissed her gently on the mouth. His hands reached for her breasts, but instead of touching her, his fingers found the zipper slide and slowly tugged it upward, drawing the two sides of her bodice together so that she was decently covered.

She stopped to swallow sudden tears. He was being so kind about this, so understanding, almost as if he knew the whole story.

Watching her, wanting her, he dropped his hands and moved aside. Sometimes, he thought, in order to hold on to a person you had to let that person go. And he very much wanted to hold on to Maura, no matter what.

Chapter Eight

After that night, she didn't see Xan for days. Still, he lodged in her thoughts the way a pebble lodges in a shoe—a discomfort, but not a disabling one. The thought of him and of that night in his bedroom was distracting, and she didn't like being distracted.

It wasn't as though she didn't have enough to keep her busy. There was the McNeill Birth Center, with curious women dropping by to find out exactly what services Maura offered, then signing up for nutrition or exercise classes. There was Golden, whose willing hands and happy spirit Maura came to depend upon. There was Kathleen, who dropped in periodically to reassure herself that Maura *really* wanted to stay in Shuffletown and *really* did not wish to return to the pleasures and comforts of Teoway Island.

One day Kathleen stopped by to deliver a letter from their parents. It was the first one Maura had received from them since she'd written them care of general delivery in a small town near the Alaskan outpost where they were backpacking, telling them she'd left the convent. With a certain amount of dread, Maura ripped the long blue envelope open.

"What do they say?" asked Kathleen, all but peering over Maura's shoulder to read the two sheets of paper, one from Fiona and one from John.

"Wait," said Maura abstractedly, running her eyes down the lines of angular script from her mother. She blinked away sudden tears as Kathleen tugged the sheet from her hands.

Kathleen skimmed the page. "She says that whatever a daughter of hers decides to do, she's behind her one hundred percent," said Kathleen, synopsizing aloud. And then with pride, "She's proud of you for standing up to the mother superior for your right to conduct a practice in home births." Kathleen grinned at Maura. "What else would you expect from Mother? Isn't she wonderful?"

Maura caught her lower lip between her teeth and smiled a wavery smile. She sighed. "Now for Dad," she said, inclining her head to read his letter.

She began with a little choked laugh. "Dad says he never thought I ought to be in that convent in the first place and that he hopes I'll have a little fun and not feel that I have to run all over the United States providing home births to everyone who wants one. And that he can't figure out why I'm so fascinated with pregnancy and deliveries, anyway; is it because my mother wasn't pregnant all the time like every other woman we knew? It wasn't her fault she had an operation that put her out of commission, he says. And why don't I hop in my van and meet him and Mother in Anchorage so we can—"

By this time Kathleen was laughing out loud. "Does he really say all that?"

Beginning to laugh herself, Maura handed the letter over. "Besides sounding really rabid about the convent, he can't possibly know what state my poor van is in, or he'd never suggest that I attempt a trip to Alaska in it. Anchorage, for goodness' sake!" And the two of them collapsed in each other's arms until their howls of mirth faded into hiccups, at least on Kathleen's part.

Then Maura folded her parents' letters, replaced them in the envelope and said soberly, "It's good to know I have their support, you know. There was a nun, Mary Szemski, who left the convent the year before I did. We heard that her family disowned her—they considered her leaving the convent a disgrace."

This made Kathleen look more serious, too. But then she brightened. "The letters from Mother and Dad made me forget my other errand, which is to tell you that a friend of mine has hired Annie Bodkin as a part-time maid."

"That's welcome news! Come on upstairs to my sitting room and tell me all about it."

They both traipsed up the wooden stairs to the sitting room, where Kathleen looked around uncomfortably and said, "Sitting room isn't exactly the right term for this place. Haven't you noticed, Maura, that there is no furniture in here?"

Maura tossed her head impatiently. "Sit on that windowsill, then, just for a few minutes. I have some photographic slides I need to sort for a presentation on home births I'm giving here tonight, and then we'll go downstairs." She pulled a box of slides from a closet shelf and sat on the floor to cull selected ones and put them in another box.

Kathleen found a perch on the windowsill as Maura set about arranging her slides. She filled Maura in on Annie Bodkin's new job and then asked, "Are you expecting a large group for your presentation tonight?"

"I've posted flyers in many local gathering places and, well, I'm hoping," said Maura.

"I can't imagine what Xan Copeland is thinking about your approach to his patients," remarked Kathleen. She watched Maura as she bent over the boxes, her face hidden from view.

Maura's position allowed her to rearrange her facial expression before she spared Kathleen a too-casual look. "He's probably wishing they'd never heard of me," she said. "I saw two expectant mothers yesterday who were Xan's patients. They're going to switch over to me. He can't be too happy about that."

Kathleen's forehead wrinkled into tight little lines. "Maura, is it absolutely necessary to take Xan's patients away?"

Maura flipped the slides backward in their box. "I'm not taking them. They come of their own accord. Women today—even the women in Shuffletown—are more conscious of themselves and their bodies than ever before, and they want to involve themselves in the birth experience. They like what I'm offering, and believe me, they're better off with me." She knew she sounded testy, but she couldn't help it.

Kathleen twisted a loose thread on the buttonhole at her wrist. "I saw Xan last weekend," she ventured finally.

"Oh?" Maura hefted the box of slides. She stood up and dusted off the seat of her blue jeans. "Come on, we can go downstairs now."

Kathleen clattered down the stairs in Maura's wake. "Xan said to tell you that he's ready and willing to take you shopping for furniture. All you have to do is give him a call. And I must agree," she said with a glance over her shoulder at the bare sitting room, "that you do need furniture."

Maura pulled a table out from the wall in the former living room and set the box of slides on it. She removed the projector from a nearby cupboard and began to adjust it.

"Well?" prompted Kathleen. "Will you?"

"Will I what?" asked Maura.

"Call Xan. He seemed. . .anxious." That was the only way Kathleen could think of to describe him. Actually, there had been more than that. Xan had looked troubled when he'd spoken of Maura, despite the fact that he was escorting a glitzy platinum blonde with eyebrows plucked to fine lines whose every action seemed calculated to impress him. And although he had been attentive to his date, he had seemed somehow absent, as though his thoughts lingered elsewhere.

"I don't know if I'll call him or not. Perhaps." Maura plugged in the projector and walked to the other end of the room, busying herself with the placement of the screen.

Kathleen sat in one of the metal folding chairs lined up in rows for the presentation. "Did something happen between you and Xan that night at his villa?"

Maura stopped fiddling with the screen and put her hands on her hips, regarding Kathleen with affectionate exasperation. "Do you think that's really any of your business?"

"I worry about you, that's all. Do you have any idea how many hours I lie awake at night, wondering how an ex-nun is going to make it in the real world?" Kathleen appeared to be joking, but there was real concern underlying her words.

Maura sighed. "He doesn't know I'm an ex-nun. And that, I suppose, is what happened that night."

"Oh. So when you were exchanging your life stories, you conveniently managed to omit ten years of your life?"

"It wasn't exactly like that," she said. "I told him about being a nurse and becoming a midwife, but I could hardly throw in all the difficulties I had in California with the convent hierarchy and the mother superior. I don't think he would have understood."

"Not many men would understand going into a convent in the first place, much less leaving one. Just think about Dad's reaction," remarked Kathleen tartly. "You'd better figure out a way to tuck the information into your conversation with a date, though."

Maura sank down into a chair beside her sister, sitting sideways and resting one arm on the back. "Kathleen, it isn't that easy. There we were on the deck of Xan's oceanside villa, the candlelight glowing, the sea singing background music, everything highly romantic. Don't you think it would have been a mood dampener if I had swung into my tale of woe about Sister Angela's being assaulted on the street and my subsequent argument with the mother superior when she ordered me to discontinue my outreach practice because she feared for my life? Anyway, it was definitely no time for Xan to find out that he was staring dreamily into the eyes of a woman fresh out of a nunnery."

"So when are you going to tell him?"

Maura sighed. "I don't know," she said unhappily. "I'm uncomfortable talking about it, you know. Aside from my own sadness over the whole episode, I think Xan might find the fact that I'm an ex-nun—well, upsetting." She bit the inside of her lip, thinking about it.

"Maura, I hardly think that being the first man in the life of an ex-nun would be upsetting," Kathleen said gently. "Perhaps Xan would even feel honored."

"Honored," said Maura thoughtfully. "I don't know. I don't know Xan that well."

"I have an idea you're going to get to know him a lot better," said Kathleen.

Maura thought for a moment and then said soberly, "Kath, you were right about how naive I was. I thought it would be easy to maintain my emotional and physical distance from Xan. But it isn't easy at all. In fact relating to a man, letting all those emotions out, is kind of like opening Pandora's box.''

Kathleen's eyes conveyed sympathy and understanding. ''I know. And with our rigid upbringing, living in these modern times isn't the way we thought it would be. You'll work out your own solutions eventually, though, just like all the rest of us.''

''I'm beginning to think of it as a reordering of my priorities. I used to think of myself as a nun first, then a nurse-midwife. There wasn't room for me. But now I find that Maura McNeill, the woman, comes before everything else. Isn't it strange?'' Maura's brown eyes seemed to brim over in wonder at this new phase of self-discovery.

Kathleen smiled. ''I don't think it's strange at all. I think it's beautiful.''

Maura smiled back, basking in her newfound grace. ''So do I,'' she said.

XAN ARRIVED THAT NIGHT after the slide presentation, totally surprising Maura. She had said good-bye to the last of her guests, turning to Golden as the last one disappeared into the darkness. Thunder rumbled in the distance, and her guests had been in a hurry to beat the rain home, since many of them had walked.

''I think the slide presentation went well, don't you, Golden?'' Maura asked her assistant, who was on her way to the kitchen carrying a half-empty pitcher of lemonade.

"Very well," said Golden. "Most of the women were surprised that you're going to be leading yoga classes for pregnant women, and I know they're interested in flavoring their food with herbs from your herb garden. All that bacon fat they use for seasoning isn't good for their health, but they've been cooking food with bacon fat all their lives and don't know any better."

"They'll learn," said Maura confidently. And then she drew in her breath sharply as she saw Xan.

He stood on the porch peering through the screen door, the brisk wind ruffling his hair over his forehead. He looked ill at ease and out of place.

"Why, Xan," she said, taking in the tall shape of him, the glint of his dark hair in the overhead porch light, the eyes that spoke his instant delight in seeing her again.

"Just checking out the competition," he said. "Am I welcome?"

"You're very welcome," she replied, her gaze steady and pleased. "Please come in."

"I can't stay," he said, following her as she led the way into the larger room. She felt his eyes upon her hips as she walked, so she turned and faced him again. But then his eyes only fell involuntarily on her breasts, and she flushed at his frank and undisguised admiration.

"I want you to come with me tonight," he said, and his voice was noncommittal and cool. She knew right away that he wasn't asking her for a date. What, then?

He grinned at the puzzlement in her eyes. "I want

you to come with me to Quinby Hospital. Sandra Giles is going to have her baby tonight. I've seen how you work, at Annie Bodkin's. Now I'd like you to see how I work."

"But I don't have delivery room privileges at Quinby," she said.

"I can get you in there. Please, Maura. It means a lot to me."

Golden slipped by, tidying the room. Maura started to help her, but Xan caught her arm as she tried to sidestep him. "Let her do that," he said softly. "We need to be at the hospital in ten minutes. We can just make it if we leave now."

"What's the point, Xan? I could get you in trouble. I don't want to interfere at Quinby."

"You'll be an observer, only an observer. How about it?" He had stopped by here on a whim; he had been desperate to see her. And he did want her to see him work. More than anything, he wanted to do something to impress her.

Observing at Quinby might give her a handle on the hospital and on Xan. Despite Dr. Urquehart's help, she still wasn't satisfied with her backup medical care. Her patients would be so much better off if they didn't have to be moved all the way to Charleston if the going got rough during a birthing. Concern for her patients' welfare won out. "I'll come," she said quickly. "As long as I'm only an observer, not a participant."

He smiled down at her. "Agreed. I didn't think you'd dare to go with me. You might find out that you approve of our methods at Quinby." His relief at her capitulation was evident.

"I'll close up the house, Maura," offered Golden.

"Thanks. I'll just get my purse and we'll go," and she ran upstairs and down again as quickly as she could.

Xan regarded her approvingly. "You're a respecter of time," he said. "I'm glad. Most women would have needed several minutes just to pull themselves together."

They walked to Xan's car through the light drizzle that had begun to fall. "I'm a midwife, remember?" she said. "I know babies don't wait."

He closed the car door after her and went around to his side and slid in. He grinned over at her, "You are so right," he said.

"Well, at least you think I'm right about something," she shot back.

"You're right about a lot of things, my dear, but your philosophy of childbirth isn't one of them."

"That's debatable," she bantered, glad that they could air their views without going for each other's throats.

"Listen, let's postpone this conversation until later," he said, reaching over and taking her hand in his. "Okay?"

Maura looked down at their clasped hands, noting his graceful fingers, the neatly clipped nails. She smiled and nodded at him, but the intent expression in his dark eyes made her look quickly away again, out at the misty night and the cotton fields flashing by the window.

Xan turned on to the Shuffletown highway and toward the hospital, the car's tires hissing on the rain-slick pavement. A thin fog wisped up at the edges of the road, curling in and out of the patches of weeds. It was only a short drive, and after Xan had parked his car in the doctors' parking lot, Maura followed him into the hospital with a sense of trepidation. Being inside a hospital again didn't feel comfortable. She wondered why she had agreed to this. She didn't belong in a hospital, not anymore.

But Xan introduced her to the delivery-room nurses without comment, explaining only that she was Maura McNeill, R.N. And then she was donning the wrinkled green pajamas that comprised standard delivery-room garb, and no one who didn't know would have guessed that Maura didn't belong.

"This is Sandra's first baby," Xan told her just before they entered the delivery room. Sandra Giles lay on the delivery table, her light-brown hair bundled up in a green cotton cap. Her blue eyes looked enormous and filled with fear. The same fear was etched across her dainty features. Maura's heart went out to Sandra immediately. She had seen too many women like this in the delivery room of the hospital where she'd worked. Frightened and dwarfed by the equipment of the delivery room, the bright lights above them, the stirrups for their feet, the strangeness of the hard table on which they lay to deliver their babies. This was one reason why Maura had become such a die-hard advocate of home births.

Maura recognized at once that the interaction between doctor and patient was special, and unusually so. In fact, as soon as he stepped into the room, something electric happened between Xan and his patient. He seemed suddenly to be charged with energy; the delivery room fairly sparked with it, and underneath it all lay Xan's basic caring and decency.

"Sandra," Xan said as soon as she saw him. His eyes twinkled at Sandra in an attempt to alleviate her almost palpable fear. "It looks as though you're about to get a birthday present, special delivery."

"Yes," she gasped, and then another contraction captured all her attention.

"Today is Sandra's birthday," he told Maura in an aside.

Maura nodded. She longed to go to the woman, to teach her how to take advantage of her breathing, to let her own calm overcome Sandra's anxiety. But Sandra was Xan's patient. According to their agreement that she was only to observe, Maura didn't dare interfere.

"My husband says that since the baby is going to be born on my birthday, we should name it after me if it's a girl," said Sandra. Her voice sounded high and tense, and she ended her sentence with a nervous little laugh.

"That's good," said Xan. "If it's a girl, that is. You'd hardly want to name a boy Sandra, would you?"

Sandra smiled weakly. "No, it will be named after my husband if it's a boy." Then another contraction took over, and Sandra concentrated on it. Maura was glad to see her concentrate. Sandra needed that focus to facilitate the birth of her baby. It was time to stop the distracting talk and get down to the business at hand. "Where is her husband?" she asked Xan quietly.

He shook his head. "He didn't take any childbirth preparation classes, so he's not allowed in the delivery room."

She nodded, but she was disappointed for Sandra's sake. This was a time that husband and wife should share, a time for understanding and sensitive spiritual growth on the part of both.

Maura saw from the patient's chart that Sandra's labor had progressed normally. Now the birth of her baby was imminent.

"All right," said Xan, taking his position at the foot of the delivery table. "Bear down now, Sandra."

Sandra did, straining mightily. She looked terribly uncomfortable to Maura, lying flat with only a pillow under her head. If she had been Maura's patient, Maura would have arranged her so that her whole torso was lifted almost to a sitting position. Maura frowned, longing to help Sandra, who was panting from exertion.

A quick assessment showed her that the baby's head was presenting. Things should move rapidly now, but Sandra was too tense. Her muscular tension at the outlet was holding the baby back. Maura swallowed, feeling Sandra's pain as a lump in her own throat. And she waited for things to get better for Sandra.

Sandra struggled through the next contraction. Xan concentrated on his job, and the other nurses were busy with their own duties. Maura was an outsider to whom they were paying no heed. She bit her lip. She wanted to do something. She knew she could help.

She couldn't help helping; she couldn't *not* do it. She touched Sandra's cheek and made eye contact, letting her know that she, Maura, was someone to be trusted. Then Maura lifted Sandra's head and shoulders so that the woman was raised into a semi-sitting position, and she slipped two more pillows beneath her.

Xan of course noted the change. For a moment his eyes, hard slivers of green glass, met Maura's over his patient. Then Sandra's body increased its force, perhaps as a result of her new position, and he had to support the just-crowned head of the baby.

Maura whispered, "You're doing beautifully, Sandra. The baby's head is crowning now."

Maura could almost feel Sandra's body surge with a new confidence as she expended her final herculean effort. For Sandra, nothing could mar the significance of her baby's birth. Anxiety and insecurity seemed to melt away, to be replaced with a new awareness. Maura exulted, too.

"It's a girl!" cried Xan, cradling the child in his hands.

"It's a girl?" gasped Sandra, exhausted.

"A beautiful baby girl, perfect in every way. A wonderful birthday present for you." Xan held the baby so that Sandra could see it.

"My baby," she said softly, her eyes shining now. "May I hold her?"

Maura would have said yes.

"No," said Xan. He handed the baby to a nurse. Sandra's eyes followed the baby, almost pathetic in their longing. The nurse efficiently began to suction the baby's mouth and nostrils.

"When can I hold her?" Sandra asked, still watching her child.

"Not for a while," Xan said cheerfully but evasively.

Maura turned away, unable to hide her disapproval. To her, maternal bonding with the infant was more important than many other considerations.

Sandra was silent then, and by the time Maura had turned back to her, Sandra's eyes were filled with tears. Her compassion for the other woman made Maura clasp Sandra's hand. She knew, from what other women had told her, that at this point Sandra felt unutterably cut off from her baby. She had carried and nurtured this baby for nine long months, and despite her relief that the baby was safely delivered, she wanted to hold it in her arms.

Sandra's eyes stayed locked on her baby throughout the ministrations of the delivery-room nurse until the child was carried through the swinging doors to the hospital nursery where, Maura knew, it would be ensconced in a plastic bassinet alongside the other babies until many hours had passed and the baby was delivered to Sandra in her hospital bed.

Xan finished up quickly. Maura continued to hold

Sandra's hand, reassuring her from time to time, all the while despairing of hospital procedure, which deprived mother and child of each other in that important time when the baby desperately needed to know of its mother's love and caring.

"So you have a new little daughter. Will you call her Sandra?" Maura talked mostly to get Sandra's mind off her baby's absence, but also to avoid confrontation with Xan, who went about his work without meeting her eyes. He wouldn't take her to task for interfering here, in the delivery room in front of the nurses and his patient. He'd wait until later, when the two of them were alone.

"My middle name is Elaine," said Sandra. "We'll probably call her that."

"Elaine Giles. A very pretty name," said Maura.

Sandra smiled. It was a proud smile, a joyful smile. "It is, isn't it? Oh, I'm so happy. So very happy."

Maura squeezed Sandra's hand. She herself didn't know the incredible happiness of giving birth, but she had experienced it vicariously hundreds of times. It never failed to leave her uplifted and filled with joy.

This time, however, her elation was soured by the knowledge that later she'd have to face up to Xan's tight-lipped disapproval of her intervention in what was supposed to have been his show.

Chapter Nine

Xan found her afterward in the staff lounge. Their eyes clashed over the top of a cardboard cup. She was drinking hot chocolate while she waited, dreading the condemnation that was sure to come. He stood glaring at her in the harshness of the fluorescent overhead light. They were separated only by a narrow table.

"Well?" he said. "Who goes first—you or me?"

"It might as well be you," she said, lowering the cup and then tossing it in a nearby trash can. She waited stoically.

"Your dislike of our methods here was quite obvious," he said, leading with a remark calculated to put her on the defensive.

"What did you expect? You know how I work," she shot back at him.

"Yes, but we'd agreed that you would be only an observer," he retorted.

"I could hardly stand by and watch Sandra suffering." She met his eyes without blinking.

Xan dismissed this assertion with a disparaging

downturn of his lips. "There's always a certain amount of pain that goes along with having a baby. It's the most easily forgotten pain in the world. I don't want my patients suffering any more than you do. But it goes with the territory." His eyes sparked with a dangerous green light.

She leaned forward on the table, resting her weight on her hands. "She didn't need to be suffering in that way. Placing pillows under her back lifted her so that the delivery could progress. I did a minor thing, but it helped. Admit it, Xan."

"Admit it? Maybe. But you should have asked my permission. You were supposed to be an *observer*, Maura."

"Then let me tell you some of the other things I observed," she said, standing up straight and preparing to count them off on her fingers. "First, Sandra was scared. Two, her fear inhibited the birth process because it made her tighten her muscles. Three, you could have relaxed those muscles by the application of hot compresses, an idea that never occurred to you. Four, she needed to hold her baby in her arms. Not wanted, but needed. Didn't you see the tears in her eyes when the nurse carted the baby off to the hospital nursery? Don't you have the compassion to see that mother and child belong together in those important first moments after birth?" Her words were impassioned. She utterly believed in them.

"Are you quite through?" he said, and his words chilled her.

"For the moment, yes. But I'll always believe that, no matter what, the beginning of a new life should be cherished."

Xan ran a hand through his hair and sighed.

"All right. Here's what I have to say. And most other obstetricians would tell you the same things."

"Go on." She had known that this airing of their professional differences was inevitable; they'd might as well get it over with.

"First, most women are apprehensive during their first experience with childbirth, and Sandra was no exception. She's heard so many horror stories and old wives' tales that she hardly knew what to expect. Second, tightened muscles or not, the birth proceeded normally and she has a fine, healthy baby. Third, there wasn't time to apply hot compresses. My delivery-room team has enough to do at such a time without wringing out wet washcloths. And fourth, it might be nice for a new mother to hold her child as soon as it's born, but hospital procedures, such as putting the silver nitrate drops in the baby's eyes to prevent disease, preclude it. Sandra had a safe delivery. That's what's important—not these cherished beginnings you're so fond of."

"What about emotions? Aren't they important to you?"

"Don't ask me about emotions! I'm a doctor, not a damned psychologist!"

"You're a doctor, not a robot! How about showing some sensitivity toward your patients?"

By this time, their exchange had become a shouting

match. A passerby peeked into the lounge, but tiptoed away when he saw what was going on.

Xan's chest heaved, and he shook his head. "It's no use, Maura. We have different views. Get your things. I'll take you home."

Her shoulders sagged. She had not convinced Xan of anything, despite her fervent speeches. He still felt that birthing was a rigid procedure, where you went by the book and followed the old rules, never minding the emotional consequences to the mother and her baby Dispiritedly she followed him as he stalked out of the room and down the lonely long hospital corridor, feeling forlorn and sad that she had failed to make Xan see things her way.

Outside, the drizzle had increased to a downpour The bright lights of the parking lot reflected from the rain-dimpled puddles on the asphalt. Xan ran through the rain to get the Cadillac, pulling it up in front of the door.

Maura climbed in, only slightly wet after her short dash to the car. She glanced at Xan from the corners of her eyes. He had gotten very wet. Rain slicked his hair across his forehead, and his eyebrows resembled wet feathers. His cotton shirt clung to his back and upper arms.

They didn't speak. Their progress was measured by the tick-swish, tick-swish of the windshield wipers. Xan drove slowly because of the heavy rain. Far away a bolt of dull lightning cut the nighttime sky, and thunder rattled the car windows.

The rain seemed to be thickening as they pulled out

on the Shuffletown highway, and soon it was so torrential that they could barely see the road ahead of them. Water gushed across the pavement, driven by the strong winds. The wind whacked the rain against the car in great sweeping gusts. Maura felt herself tensing; driving in this weather was treacherous.

"I'm going to have to pull over," said Xan tersely. "I can't drive through this."

Maura said nothing, just watched as Xan slowed the Cadillac to a complete stop. She heard the slap of wet weeds on the car's underbelly as he drove off the asphalt onto the shoulder of the road.

He touched the automatic buttons to open the front windows slightly for air, and the air felt cool and smelled like dust. Then he turned off the engine, and the windshield wipers stopped their sweeping. Finally he switched off the headlights and reached for the control that would ease the car seat backward to give them more legroom. If they had to sit there in the rain, they might as well be comfortable while they did it.

He never should have taken Maura to the hospital. He knew that now. At the time it had seemed like a good idea. He'd wanted to see her, and he didn't think she'd agree to a date with him, not after that night at his villa when it had taken all his restraint to let her go. He had known she would accompany him tonight if it had something to do with her calling, and anyway, he was proud of the way he interacted with his patients; he loved his work, loved everything about it.

He was dedicated to bringing good medical care to

the patients at the Quinby Hospital and intended to continue. He'd watched Maura deliver a baby. She had made an art of it. Well, he approached delivering babies as a science, as any good doctor would. And he was damned proud of that.

He glanced at her. She was staring at the runnels of rain creasing the windshield. His heart softened at the sight of her clean, uncluttered profile. Her head was regal on the long stem of her neck, crowned in brilliant red-gold like the daylilies in the exclusive Teoway Island flower beds. She was so unknowingly beautiful and so uncommonly self-assured. He found himself caring for her as he had cared for no other woman. His caring was built on admiration and respect and a gut feeling that the two of them were very much in tune, despite their different philosophies.

Xan cleared his throat. "Maura, about what we said back there," he began, framing an apology in his mind.

She wouldn't let him finish. "There's nothing more to be said," she told him. She wasn't cold, or even cool. She was just Maura. He would have expected her to sulk or argue. Except that that wasn't the way Maura was.

He sighed, determined to try again. "All right. We won't talk about that. When are we going to go furniture shopping?"

She swung her head around, wafting the earthy fragrance of wet hair toward him. He liked the scent of it. It reminded him of the fragrance of her skin that night in his bedroom.

"Go furniture shopping? Oh, Xan, there's no point in carrying this any further. We're on opposite sides of the childbirth issue. Let's just drop the whole relationship, all right?" Her brown eyes beseeched him.

He felt a stab of dismay. He shook his head firmly. "No, dropping the relationship is definitely not all right. I'm willing to admit that we don't see eye to eye professionally. But I'd like to see you again."

Maura let herself be drawn into the intensity of his gaze for a moment, then fought her way out of it before it sucked her under. "There's no point in it." She spoke decisively, as if there could be no argument.

He took a deep breath. "Maura, I like you very much, and it's seldom that I meet a woman as intelligent as you are. I enjoy talking with you and I'm physically attracted to you. As far as I'm concerned, there's every reason to keep the relationship going."

"I see," she said. "You have it all figured out, so very rationally. This, therefore that. I was right. You don't have any emotions."

"I damn well do have emotions," he said, beginning to get annoyed. "One of them is anger. Why do you keep accusing me of having none?"

"Because you don't show them, that's why!"

"So what do you want me to do? Tell you I'm madly in love with you? We hardly know each other, and if you get your way, we never will!"

Her nerves felt coiled tight as a spring. She let the silence grow, and after a while it no longer felt threatening. She caught her breath when he raised a finger and traced its way downward from her cheekbone to her jaw. He was looking at her with incredible longing, and she found herself wanting to experience the wonderfully delicious sensations she felt whenever she was in his arms.

Xan caressed the curve of her lower lip with the same lazy fingertip, imprisoning her eyes with his. Her lips parted reluctantly before his finger tentatively touched the tip of her tongue. She savored the taste of him, feeling the heat of her arousal spreading through her body in widening ripples. After a moment he continued the tracing of her features with his finger, bringing into being a yearning so strong that it became a growing, aching need. She closed her eyes for a moment, wanting to ease away from that need, and when she opened them he had narrowed the space between them and his lips were closing on hers.

If there was frustration inside her, it melted away as she became aware of the softness of his lips. Whatever harsh words had passed between them counted for nothing in the hazy drifting easiness of being swept away on a gentle tide of lethargy. And then gradually their heartbeats accelerated, their breath grew more frantic. Xan's kisses unleashed the passions that she had checked for so long, and they battered at her resistance like the wings of frenzied birds longing to be free. She found herself clutching at him, spanning his shoulders with spread fingers taut with the urgency of it, pressing him closer in her desperate need. And throughout the fierce craving onslaught of his kisses, she kept thinking, *this can't be happening! Not to me!*

But it was happening. Her own clothes picked up the dampness and began to cling to her skin where they touched his wet clothes, and still he held her tenaciously, his mouth eager upon hers, and savage.

While he could still think, when he first began kissing her, he thought about how long he had waited to kiss her since that last time, and how many times he had dreamed of doing it again. He wanted her, all of her, wanted to know her inch by inch. And he wanted her to know him. And then he didn't think anymore.

The rain curtained them from the rest of the world; they were encapsulated, isolated, far away from everyone else. Their breathing fogged the car windows so that they couldn't see out; it was just the two of them together.

The male textures of him were so new to her as her hands found his hair, caressing and then winding themselves into the wet strands, finding their way to curve around the nape of his neck, then traveling slowly and tantalizingly down his backbone to rest lightly at the hollow just above his hips.

His mouth released hers and burned little breathy kisses along her throat, and her lips pressed against his damp skin and tasted warm rain.

Outside, the storm lessened and the rain drummed more quietly on the roof of the car, tapering off until it was no more than a mist. With the ceasing of the storm, they felt no longer separate from but a part of the world outside.

"I know you need time, my darling," he whispered

close to her ear. "But I don't want to wait much longer."

She buried her face in his wet shoulder, and she couldn't tell if the moisture on her cheeks was rain or tears.

"Nothing to say?" he said gently, tipping her face so that he could look at it in the darkness. He wished he knew how to communicate his longing to her, to tell her how very much he wanted her.

"What if—what if I told you that it wasn't going to happen?" she breathed.

Xan said nothing for a moment, then spoke very carefully. "Then I would ask you why you are making me hurt for you. You are, you know." His eyes spoke volumes in their intensity.

He could not have said anything that would have shaken her more. She hated hurting anything ever. She knew this was a different kind of hurting. But did that make it different? For she was hurting, too—aching in want of him.

Carefully, as though she were very fragile and precious, Xan disengaged himself from her and hitched the car seat forward. Maura retreated to her own side of the seat, smoothing her hair back and not daring to look at him. He drove her home on rain-slick roads, and they did not speak even when she fumbled with the door latch and let herself out. She ran up the steps of the farmhouse and slipped inside as quickly as possible. She sank down on the stairs, overcome by her own thoughts.

A love affair would be a veering from her course,

and she was dedicated to her mission here in Shuffletown. Yet it suddenly seemed crystal clear to her that, unless something happened to stop it, she was indeed about to embark on a love affair. The aftershocks of this certain knowledge shook her for days afterward. She could not come to terms with the idea of herself as Xan's lover; she still needed time.

THE NEXT EVENING as twilight spread shadows over the cotton field behind the farmhouse, Maura put on a rust-colored leotard and unrolled a straw mat on the commodious side porch where bumblebees darted in and out of the nearby rosebushes. She planned to do some refreshing yoga exercises to clear her mind and relax her body. Then when she felt totally free of tension, she'd think about the things she had been putting off thinking about. She had just finished a series of hollow breaths, a technique that induces calmness, and was lying on her back inhaling the roses' fragrance when something furry brushed up against her feet. It meowed.

She sat up and found herself face to face with the scruffiest cat she had ever seen. It wasn't at all pretty, with its patchy gray tiger-striped fur and kinked tail. "Poor thing," she said sympathetically, reaching to scratch it behind the ear. It closed its eyes and let out a heartrending meow. "I suppose I'll have to feed you," she said. "It doesn't look as though anyone else ever does."

The footstep beside her startled her, and she looked up at Xan Copeland, who was staring down at her and the cat with a bemused expression. "If you're feeling in the mood to be kind to strays," he said, "will you take on another one? No one feeds me, either." He smiled at her engagingly, feasting his eyes on the earth tones of her spread out on the mat before him.

"I was going to feed this poor animal chicken livers. Would you like some?" There was teasing in her look, but her heart was turning over at the sight of him.

Xan grimaced. "Hardly. Don't you have some left-overs or something?" He sat down in the big double-sized rope hammock which Golden had strung up on the porch for the comfort of waiting fathers. He looked at her hungrily, and she knew he was hungry for more than dinner.

"Did you bring this cat?" she said quickly to dis-tract herself from his presence. "I didn't hear you drive up."

He nodded. "That's because we both came on little cat feet. I brought her for your mice. Remember?"

She couldn't possibly have forgotten that night. But she hadn't seen a mouse since, and she had forgotten that Xan had said he'd get her a cat. "She's such a sad specimen," she said, her heart going out to the poor thing. "Where did you ever find her?" Concentrating on the cat made it possible for her to dismiss the depth of Xan's eyes, which made his feelings for her so very obvious.

"I found her hanging around the garbage cans out-side the hospital. Considering her condition, I thought she needed the services of the McNeill Birth Center."

He was right. The cat's sides were bulging, a sure sign of an advanced pregnancy. Maura stopped rubbing the purring cat behind the ears and stood up quickly. Right now she'd welcome an activity, any activity. "Come on, both of you. I'll see what I can find in the refrigerator. Beggars, however, can't be choosers." She bent and picked up the cat, cradling its ample body between her breasts.

Xan tipped himself out of the hammock and followed her inside to the kitchen. Maura opened the refrigerator door. "There's leftover spaghetti, cooked and mixed with sauce, if you'd like that."

"Sounds wonderful. Do you know that's the ugliest cat I've ever seen? It looks boneless, too."

Maura regarded the cat, which was focusing yellow unblinking eyes upon her face. "You're right."

"I hope you know something about birthing kittens."

"I think cats take care of those things themselves," she said, setting the cat on the floor, where it proceeded to twine through their legs, purring in anticipation. Maura found the chicken livers and set them down in a bowl. The cat began to gulp them down voraciously.

"Speaking of birthing," said Xan slowly as Maura dumped the cold cooked spaghetti into a pan to warm it, "the chief of staff at the hospital, Raymond Lyles, called me into his office today."

"Oh?" Maura kept her eyes on the spaghetti.

"Dr. Lyles asked me my opinion about setting up a birthing room in the hospital. And he mentioned giving family-oriented childbirth care, complete with midwife labor coaches.''

She glanced at him, eyebrows raised. "What brought this big change about?" she asked.

Xan leaned against the wall, watching her as she stirred the spaghetti. "He's been visited by some of the Teoway Island women, who want to know why Quinby Hospital doesn't offer alternative birthing methods. It seems that one of the women employs Annie Bodkin as a maid, and Annie has been singing your praises loud and clear.''

Maura stopped stirring and stared at Xan in amazement.

"Anyway, these women—most of them patients of mine—would like to try home births, but they're angry that they'd have to rely on a hospital twenty miles away in case of emergency. Raymond is feeling the pressure.''

The two of them sat down at the kitchen table with their plates of spaghetti.

"So setting up a birthing room is Dr. Lyles's way of appeasing these women?''

"He's conscientious about providing the best in health care for Quinby Hospital patients. He wants a midwife to work as a labor coach in the new birthing room at first. It looks as though it might be an in for you.''

"What kind of an in?"

"Eventually, delivery-room privileges. Emergency-room privileges. Everything you need and want, and not twenty miles away in Charleston, but right here in Shuffletown.''

Then it was as though a light bulb flashed on inside her head. She eyed Xan with suspicion. "Say, how much did you have to do with this?"

He chewed his spaghetti slowly, a gleam in his eye. "What makes you think I had anything to do with it?"

"A certain remark you made about it being worth getting me on the staff of Quinby Hospital so that we could at least run into each other occasionally in the staff lounge."

"You have to admit it would be one way to see more of each other." He watched her carefully, but he didn't like the way her cheeks were coloring.

"Xan, I told you I don't want to work in a hospital. And I certainly don't want to be a mere labor coach when I'm already handling my own deliveries." She set her fork down very carefully beside her plate and stared at him.

"I know you said you don't want to work in a hospital, but—"

"And I meant it. My kind of midwifery works best in a home environment." Her words were clipped short.

"Maura, you're getting so angry, and I really don't understand why," he said patiently. She was overreacting. Even though he knew she wanted to birth babies only in her patients' homes, he had thought that she would welcome this way of gaining privileges at Quinby Hospital. To tell the truth of it, the birthing room had seemed like a solution to the problem of getting to see more of Maura, but it hadn't been his idea. It had been his patients' idea, just as he'd told her.

"Why are you so angry about this?" he asked.

Memories flooded over Maura. "Because—because I decided at a certain point in my career that I should only work with families in their homes. I had to—to choose my kind of midwifery over the kind practiced in a hospital, subject to all the requisite rules and regulations of an institution." Leaving a surprised Xan staring after her, she stood up abruptly and ran outside. Suddenly the kitchen seemed stifling. She needed fresh air.

Totally perplexed, Xan jumped up from the table, almost knocking his chair over in haste. He followed Maura into the backyard, where she stood beneath a hickory tree staring out over the straight green rows of the cotton field beyond. She was trembling slightly when he put his arms around her, as though she would run away any minute.

"All right, sweetheart," he said gently, cuddling her close, feeling her heart drumming against his chest. "Do you want to talk about it?"

A hesitation. Then she shook her head no. But her heart's pounding lessened.

He tipped her face toward his and saw great sadness there. He had seen it before, when she had been thinking about the other man, the one in California who had hurt her so. Yet at this moment he was sure that tonight's sorrow had nothing to do with that boyfriend of hers. This had to do with something else.

Wanting desperately to reassure her, hoping that she would open up and tell him what was on her mind, he said against her hair, "I cupped a wild bird in my hand once. It felt like you do—tense, its little heart beating away against its feathers.''

"What happened?" she said unsteadily.

"I opened my hand and it flew away."

"I don't want to fly away." Indeed, her heart had slowed and she felt less like flinging herself away into the darkness of the night

He waited, but she didn't speak. His arms tightened around her. "I guess I insulted you by suggesting that you work as a labor coach," he said, treading carefully, hoping she would talk to him, really talk to him about what was upsetting her. There were depths to her that he had never fully understood, would never understand until she trusted him enough to talk about them.

When she remained silent, he said, "I thought you might not mind working in the birthing room for a while if it meant eventual backup for your patients so much closer to home."

Her patients. She should be thinking of them first, not herself. It would be traumatic to do labor coaching in a hospital, and she didn't like the rigid delivery-room methods at Quinby. But Xan was right—she had her patients to consider.

She pulled away from Xan, keeping a tight hold on his hand. "I don't want to be just a labor coach," she said. "But I might consider it if it would benefit my patients in the end. What do you want me to do?"

They began to stroll back toward the house.

"Perhaps you could talk with Raymond Lyles. See what kind of arrangement he has in mind. After all, the birthing-room concept is new at Quinby."

They walked up the steps to the porch, and Xan opened the kitchen door for her. "I'll think about it, Xan," she said thoughtfully.

"That's good enough for now," he told her, relieved.

"Would you be my medical supervisor?" She riveted her eyes on him.

"Ah, Maura, the first time I ever saw you deliver a baby so artfully, I knew you had a gift for it. I have the utmost respect for your expertise. It—it's just hard for me to overcome the prejudice most obstetricians harbor against midwives."

"Does that mean yes or no?"

"I guess," he hedged, nonetheless smiling down at her, "that it means a definite maybe. Couldn't we discuss it more thoroughly after you've talked with Raymond?"

"I suppose so," she conceded, realizing that they were still skirting the issue but finding it unimportant to press it at this point.

He pulled her into his arms. "That makes two definite maybes," he said, smiling against her hair.

She smiled, too. "Now that we've got all that over with, I think we should eat our dinner."

"Guess what?" he said. He was facing the kitchen table; her back was to it. He could see it; she couldn't.

"What?" she replied. She could feel his eyes looking at something over the top of her head.

"We're too late."

She wheeled around and saw the cat sitting brazenly

on the tablecloth washing her paws. Both of their plates had been licked clean.

"I didn't know cats ate spaghetti," she said. She went to the table and scooped the cat up, setting her carefully on the floor.

"Spaghetti is the one thing all pregnant cats crave," Xan said seriously. "Like pickles and ice cream, or strawberries in the wintertime for pregnant women."

"How do you..." and then she realized he was joking.

After they had scrounged leftover ham from the refrigerator and eaten hastily assembled sandwiches, while they were cleaning up and the cat had been put out, Maura said with some embarrassment, "I'd invite you to sit with me in my parlor, but I've been so busy that I haven't bought any furniture yet."

"Still no furniture? But that's ridiculous! How can we sit and spoon if there's no place to sit?" Xan stared at her in mock astonishment.

"We'll sit on the front porch," she said hastily.

They didn't, however, get that far. The electronic pager Xan always wore on his belt went off just as they reached the door. One of his patients was about to deliver, and he had to rush to the hospital.

"Sorry," he said in exasperation. "It looks as though this means another evening is lost to us."

Her disappointment was monumental. "I'm glad you stopped by," she said, meaning it.

"Me, too," said Xan. He bent and kissed her lightly upon the lips, and her lips tingled where his had touched them. Her mind whirled dizzily with the knowledge that if Xan had stayed, she would more than likely have had to decide whether or not they would finally become lovers She would have been confronted again with his forceful and skillful lovemaking and would have had to either call a halt or

But now a decision was not necessary, had been taken out of her hands by fate or nature or whatever. Maura didn't know whether to be happy or sad, but if the truth were to be told, she felt more like crying than laughing. What did that mean?

Unaware of her ambivalence, he said, "I'll see you soon."

Maura slid her arms up around his neck, closing her eyes and resting her head for a moment on his shoulder. It felt solid. It felt good. Everything about him felt right. She was only human, with very human desires and urges. So why couldn't she accept a sexual relationship with Xan? She wanted him. Oh, yes, she wanted him every bit as much as he wanted her But there was something, some last bit of restraint that made her hold back.

THE NEXT DAY Xan solved the problem of their never having time to be together in a unique way. He kidnapped her. It wasn't a kidnapping in the usual sense of the word, but he wouldn't take no for an answer He arrived at the McNeill Birth Center in midmorning, a morning bright as a promise.

In the front yard, Maura and Golden were picking up dead twigs and branches that the wind had blown out of the pecan trees. The stray cat, who apparently knew a good thing when she found it and had decided to stay, was pouncing playfully on anything that moved. Maura straightened when Xan's motorcycle charged into the driveway. "Xan!" she said. "Aren't you supposed to be working today?"

"I've already made my hospital rounds, and I'm entitled to vacation days now and then, you know," he said, gunning his motor. He grinned at her, his teeth white against his tan. "Come out with me. We'll find you some furniture."

"I have work to do," she said.

"No, you don't," said Golden firmly. "This is Saturday, and you don't have any checkups scheduled, or exercise classes either. I'm on call all weekend in case somebody decides to be born. And I can pick up these branches by myself. You go."

Xan turned off his Honda's motor and rested the motorcycle on its kickstand. "We'll take your van," he said, appropriating the burlap bag into which Maura had been tossing broken branches. He slung the bag toward Golden with a wink. Then he grasped Maura firmly by the hand and led her to the van.

"I can't do this!" protested Maura, smoothing at her hair. "I'm not ready to go anywhere. I'm wearing old clothes. Let me go, Xan!"

"No," he said firmly, opening her van's passenger door and boosting her up with hands around her waist. "We're not going any place fancy. But you do need furniture, and I need you. So it's best for us to fulfill our needs together, wouldn't you say?" He grinned at her again, this time mischievously, before he ran around the van and got in the driver's side. The keys were in the ignition.

In a few moments they were zinging along the Shuffletown highway, and she was laughing over at him in disbelief. "All right, Xan Copeland, where are we going?" She couldn't be angry with him, not when he was grinning at her like that. The day suddenly seemed to be infused with a new happiness, and Maura realized all at once that there was no place she would rather be at that moment than at Xan's side, no matter where he was taking her.

"We're going right here," he said, steering the van into a muddy parking lot beside an unpainted cinder-block building. "It doesn't look like much, but the fellow does upholstery work and sometimes he has a bargain or two sitting around. Now, if I'm not mistaken, you need a couch, right?"

Maura nodded agreement, and inside Xan routed the proprietor from the back room and found out that the man had two couches for sale, both left for re-upholstering and both unclaimed by the owners.

"Which one do you like?" asked Xan.

One was red tweed and ghastly, the other moss-green velvet and gorgeous. Xan spread his long length out on the green one, to Maura's great embarrassment, and pronounced it comfortable. In minutes he and the proprietor had loaded it into the back of the van.

"Was that so bad? Now you and Kathleen will have a place to sit when you have your sisterly tête-à-têtes," said Xan when they were back on the highway.

"So you've been talking to Kathleen," said Maura.

"Not entirely true. Kathleen has been talking to me," he said.

"Betraying sisterly confidences, no doubt," said Maura wryly.

"Not at all. Unless telling me to hurry up and go shopping with you or she would take you shopping herself qualifies as a sisterly confidence."

"It probably doesn't," said Maura, relieved. "She knows I hate shopping. Where are we going now?"

"To a nice little lady who deals in antiques and refinishes furniture on the side. She may have some occasional tables you'll like."

Maura laughed. "When did you plan this? You've really thought all of it out."

"I have been planning this for a long time, my dear. Do you suppose I like to think of your living in a house that isn't really a home? You should be surrounded by your own meaningful possessions."

"Oh, I don't want a lot of possessions," she told him seriously. "But I do like to have beauty around me, something pretty."

Fans of a smile wrinkled the edges of his eyes, and he looked at her fondly. "So do I, Maura. And you're it."

Under Xan's tutelage she found two small tables for her living room, one inlaid walnut and the other solid cherry, and an original framed watercolor by the Charleston artist Elizabeth O'Neill Vernor for her upstairs hall. By late afternoon, when they had a vanload of furniture and related items, Xan suggested that they not push their luck with Maura's van, which had chugged gamely along for hours.

"I think we should call it quits," he said, "because I'm hungry. Aren't you?"

"Slightly," she said, and at that precise moment her stomach rumbled and betrayed her hunger.

He coaxed the van southward along U.S. 17 and down an obscure byway to the Shrimpboat, a tiny restaurant miles down the coast and overlooking a dock in a sheltered cove where shrimp trawlers moored. It was a local restaurant, unknown to all but the people who lived in that tiny coastal town and a privileged few others.

They feasted on jumbo boiled shrimp that had just been caught that morning, and Xan peeled the first shrimp for her and put it into her mouth, a sensory pleasure to be sure. And then he explained how to make perfect cocktail sauce — "use fresh-grated horse-radish and just the right amount of bottled chili sauce—the secret is all in the proportions—and then add three drops of fresh lemon juice" — and he promised to make his own cocktail sauce for her the next time she came to his villa for dinner if she'd never, ever give away the secret. He was charming, absolutely charming, and she wondered why it had taken her so long to slip out from under that invisible nun's habit she'd worn as a shield for so long after she'd arrived here. But she had done it—she'd finally opened herself to her new life and all its possibilities. And she had done it with Xan's help.

As she watched the boats slipping one by one into

the cove, heavy with the day's catch of shrimp and gilded by the afternoon sunlight, with Xan sitting across from her so animated and so solicitous of her own happiness, she thought her heart would burst with the knowledge that she had denied now for much too long. She looked at him, helpless to control her feelings, and she marveled that in such a short time he had become someone with whom she felt so at peace, so natural, so at one. And it seemed that she could no longer silence herself.

Maura never recalled afterward what he had been saying at that moment, although she would never forget the deep emerald green of his eyes, or the way his lips curved upward into a half smile as he spoke, or the oddly incongruous bump in the middle of his nose.

"I never meant to fall in love!" she blurted, interrupting him in midsentence.

Xan didn't speak for a long moment, just delved into the depths of her eyes with his, the love in his eyes warm and genuine and unfaltering. Then he smiled and reached across the red-checkered tablecloth to cover her hand reassuringly with his own. "I'm afraid, my darling, that it's too late to do anything about it," he said with utter sincerity, and he tenderly lifted her hand to his lips and kissed it gently on the palm.

Chapter Ten

They didn't discuss it; there was no need to talk about it in words. They communicated with a look, a touch, a silent subtle signaling of body language. It was tacitly understood by both of them that Maura would go home with Xan to his villa that night.

They drew up in his driveway in her van, caught up in the magic of the starlit night. Tonight Maura felt joyfully alive and new, on the threshold of something glorious. Xan had made her feel special in the eyes of another person for the first time in her life, and very much a woman.

He didn't rush her. "Come with me," he said leading her around the villa to the dunes. They walked to the top of one high dune and looked out at the star-silvered ocean ruffling in glittering wavelets toward shore. As they watched, two deer, a doe and her fawn, daintily picked their way out of the dark dunes and stood listening intently at the water's edge. Then the two animals leisurely picked their way around a series of tide pools down the beach before disappearing out of sight.

"I've seen those two deer before," said Xan. "They are totally unafraid of man. I guess they know they're protected here on the island and have nothing to fear."

Maura rested her head on Xan's shoulder, lifting her face to brush his cheek with her lips. "I wish we could swim," she said. "The water looks so cool and inviting."

"We can swim if you like," replied Xan.

"But—"

"Let's not just stand here talking about it. It's time for action, not words!" With that he tugged at her hand, and laughing back at her, delighted with the astonished expression on her face, he pulled her down the grassy slope of the dune lickety-split until they stopped hand in hand at the edge of the sea.

"Kick your shoes off," he ordered, slipping his off and dropping them in a patch of dried seaweed. She did as she was told, reveling in the spontaneity of it.

And then Xan swung her up into his arms, lifting her as though she were feather-light, his eyes exploring the depths of hers. He waded into the ocean deeper, deeper, until the water reached his knees, his hips, and then the waves rose enticingly bit by bit to lap at her body, which was still cradled in his arms.

"Didn't we forget something?" she murmured against his chest, feeling the salt spray misting against her cheek.

"Did we?" he said, his lips close to her ear.

"We didn't take our clothes off," she said, tilting her head so that she could look at him and see the expression on his face.

Xan was still amused, still enjoying the moment, but there was something deeper in his expression as well. He slowly released her so that her body slid into the water against the long length of his, touching him all the way down as she found her footing on the sand below.

"No one ever swims fully clothed," he said, his arms flowing out and around her and pulling her tightly against him. Maura could feel him, all of him, the only barrier between their eager bodies layers of wet cloth. The ocean currents swirled around them, unbelievably sensuous in their caress, rendering her unsteady on her feet. She clutched at him for support, catching her breath for one heart-stopping moment as skin electrified skin. But she had already made her choice; she would not change her mind.

Her fingers tugged at the buttons on his shirt. She pushed the first one through its hole, but the rhythmic undulating motion of the waves made it difficult to unbutton the second. She fumbled for a moment, and he caught her up close to him. They supported each other, swaying against the playful currents as she unbuttoned the third.

His tongue traced the vulnerable line from her chin to her ear, licking the salt from her skin. She drew in her breath sharply.

"Let me help," he said, gently covering her fingers with his.

"No," she whispered. "I want to do this."

Xan surrendered his clothes to her then, concentrating on pleasuring her with his lips and teeth and tongue, finding her eyelids, her nose, her ears, her lips as she carefully undid the buttons of his shirt. He could hardly stand the pleasure of her willing touch, the pain of waiting for more.

The sight of his chest, the springy hairs damp and whorled into a new pattern by the waves, took her breath away. He shrugged out of the shirt, and when it slipped through her fingers into the sea, he said, "Let it go."

Her lips sought his, her arms reaching up, up, until her fingers wove themselves through his hair. "Oh, Maura," he sighed against her lips, and his kiss was excruciatingly sweet as their lips parted, their tongues touched, and she trembled with the joy of it.

Maura's hands glided to his waist, sliding around the snug wet waistband of his pants. His lips released her even as his eyes imprisoned her in their passion, and they never left hers as she undid the fastener and lowered the zipper slowly and carefully beneath the surface of the dark water. With one quick motion he stepped out of the pants, letting them flow into the current, and she tugged at his underwear until his magnificent body sprang free. She touched him carefully, gently, exploring him in wonder.

He moaned softly. Her fingers elicited the most delicious sensations, but he couldn't let her go on doing that without doing something for her in return. He slipped his hands around her slender waist and up until her sensitive breasts filled his hands. They were so round, so full, and their swollenness betrayed her desire. As usual, she wore no brassiere, and the thought of her beautiful upthrust breasts unbound within his hands excited him so that he suddenly twisted the sides of her blouse, tearing the thin fabric in his eagerness to touch her warm skin.

"It's all right," she said shakily. "These are old clothes." He ripped the garment away, his eyes marveling at the newly revealed beauty and perfection of her. His fingertips tentatively touched the very peaks, teasing them until they gathered into tight round tips. Waves licked at the undersides of her breasts, gentling the sensitive bottom curves, sucking into the hollow between them.

Maura had never known that her body was so full of points of pleasure; parts of her body that she had never given much heed suddenly became all-important. Her shoulders, where his lips dropped hot kisses; her earlobes, branded by his tongue; her forehead, pressed tightly against his cheek.

Maura rejoiced at the titillating sensation of skin against skin, of her moist nipples tipping through his wet body hair. Her whole body ached and glowed and cried out for more, for all.

His hands feathered languidly down the sides of her breasts and skimmed to her waist, finally reaching the snap on her jeans, where they hesitated. This was the time when, if she wanted to, she could stop him. But she didn't.

"Shall I?" he said, his breath hot against her forehead.

"Yes, Xan," she cried, shaken by her own desire. She closed her eyes, wishing that he would hurry. If he hadn't supported her with one hand against the steady billowing of the waves, Maura would surely have fallen. Then he unsnapped the jeans and she was stepping out of them, letting them go, glad to be free of their heavy wet constraint.

His hands curved around her hips, drawing her closer until she felt the magnitude of his desire surging against her belly. Caressingly he pulled down the wisp of lace that covered her and let it float away into the current like a bit of sea foam.

She could never have imagined such eroticism as she felt now with Xan, naked against him beneath the waves. He pulled her close to him and held her as their hearts synchronized; he was supporting her, loving her, infusing her with longing.

"My darling Maura," he said softly into the damp swirling cloud of her hair. "I love you so much. I've never loved anyone like this. Never."

Her arms slid up around him in silent surrender, and her body rocked against his with an awareness that was pure instinct.

He knelt before her in the water, his head held barely above the glassy surface, his mouth suckling at one breast until she sighed, almost a moan. One hand around her slick swaying hips pressed her to him, and always there was the susurrus of the sea, swelling and ebbing in the small space between them. She wrapped one leg around his body for support, and then he stood in one fluid motion, water streaming off him in star-spun rivulets, and there were no waves between them at all.

His body throbbed against her, and he commanded, "Put your other leg around me."

She did, and then was amazed that his seeking fingers were so gentle and so knowing in her warm secret places. "Oh," she cried out, her cry wafted away on the sea wind. "Oh, Xan, I love you. Love me. Love me." And her plea was almost a sob.

"My God, you're a passionate woman, Maura." He had not thought she would be ready so soon, but she was. He had meant to love her here for only a little while, a fervent and romantic starlit prelude to their tumultuous coupling later in his big, high bed. But she was clearly longing for fulfillment, and he had waited so long that he was nearly frantic with his own need.

He lifted her hips to settle her upon him, the water providing its own sensuous caress. Gently he probed her moist tightness, holding back his passion, wanting to be careful with her, wanting to bring her maximum pleasure. He could not believe it when he met resistance.

"Maura?" he whispered, leaning back to look at her face. Her eyes met his, and in them was the truth. The knowledge staggered him. He could not believe she had never made love before.

"Please, Xan," she whispered urgently, "I want you to."

"But you've never..."

She hid her face in his shoulder and clung to him with all her might.

"Oh, my darling," he said quietly. "You should have told me." His arms enfolded her, pressed her to

him. He felt strong and sturdy and utterly supportive.
She began to shiver, holding fast to his strength.

Holding her, his mind racing, wondering how she
could still be untouched when he was almost certain
she'd had an unhappy love affair in California, Xan's
desire faded. Tenderness took its place. Carefully, so
that she would know he was not rejecting her, he let
her go. Her feet found their place on the sand, but no
sooner had they settled there than he was lifting her in
his arms, cuddling her to his wide chest.

"What are you doing?" she said, her voice shaking.
Had she disappointed him? What had she done
wrong?

"I'm taking you into the house," he said firmly,
striding out of the ocean, the seawater sluicing from
their bodies in streams.

The beach was deserted, and there was no one to
mark their rapid traversing of the sand to Xan's villa.
He kicked open a door, refusing to put her down, and
he marched, both of them still naked and dripping, up
the stairs to the second floor. He strode to the bedroom, where he laid her gently on the coverlet of the
big, high rice bed that had bred generations of Cope-
lands. And then he laid himself on top of her, covering her body with his own so that she wouldn't be
cold.

"Xan?" she said, searching his face for whatever
emotions—disgust, disappointment, anger—he was
feeling.

"My sweet, lovely Maura," he said, securing her
head between his two hands so that she couldn't

move it, and then his lips descended upon hers, kissing her so thoroughly and yet so sensitively that she felt that kiss in the great pulsing center of her, banishing all thought.

When he had finished kissing her, Maura opened her eyes to see his face limned in the moon glow filtering through the narrow wooden blinds. "You're not taking birth control pills? You're not protected?" he asked.

Birth control pills?

"No, I—" she said, realizing that she should have anticipated this.

"Don't worry," he said gently. "I'll take care of it."

She pulled his head to her breast, stroking his hair softly, her fingers lightly caressing the pulse point at his temple. His body no longer felt alien to her or strange. It seemed right, now, that it finally be a part of her.

He looked down at her in wondering adoration. "If it's your first time, darling, I want you to feel it in a special way. I want you to be satisfied. Are you afraid?"

"Not afraid," she told him, her words a mere whisper. "Worried that I won't please you."

He kissed her nose, her chin, the hollow of her throat. "I won't hurt you," he promised. "And you'll please me. But this won't be the only time, you know. So don't try too hard. Just let it happen."

His words eased her apprehension. "I didn't want you to know I've never done this before," she confessed, her eyes dark with love. "I wanted you to think I was just like everyone else. That I knew all the things..."

He trailed a long feathery string of kisses down her neck, her chest, her breast until she trembled with need of him. He stopped to circle her nipple gently with his tongue, and she felt the sensation deep inside her, and with it came the joy that her emptiness was finally going to be filled.

"You do know all the things," he told her. "With you, it will be natural and real and right," and his arms clasped her to him and he held her for a long time, silently communicating the depth of his happiness until his body began to pulse with desire.

"Oh, Xan," she said, overwhelmed with her certain love for him as his hands began again to explore her intimate crevices with the most tantalizing languor. "I was meant for this moment."

"You were meant to be mine," he said unsteadily, and then, slowly and reverently and with more love than lust, he set about making her really and truly his in body as well as in spirit.

LATER XAN WATCHED MAURA as she slept, her hair cascading over the pillowcase like a spill of bright rubies, and he wondered how it was that he, that very night, had been the first man in her life.

Twenty-eight. She was twenty-eight years old. And the pain in her eyes when she spoke of her previous life in California had been real. She must have had someone; she was too beautiful and too passionate to have remained alone all this time. But then how...?

He wouldn't ask her about it, that was for sure. It would be no good if he had to drag it out of her; he wanted her to trust him enough to tell him everything. He'd work on that trust, and when she felt wrapped securely in their love for each other, she'd talk to him. Why bring up the past if it would only cause her mental anguish? They loved each other, that was all that mattered. He could wait until she was ready to tell him all the secrets she held in her heart.

He drew her close to him, and she stirred in her sleep with a contented sigh and nestled her head more comfortably on his shoulder. He gently rearranged her hair so that it spread across his chest like a silken coverlet. Then he kissed her once very lightly on the forehead, buried his face in her fragrant hair, and fell asleep.

Early in the morning, just as the sun's first opal rays burst from the horizon, his bedside telephone rang. Xan managed to grab it on the first ring.

"Mrs. Jameson? All right. Sure. I'll be right there."

Maura groped for him, touched his chest. He hung up and lifted her hand to his lips, kissing the tips of her fingers one by one. Then he swung his feet around and sat on the edge of the bed. "Nancy Jameson is about to deliver. I need to hurry over to the hospital," he told her, smoothing his hand along her flat abdomen and touching her lightly on the breast.

Her eyes opened and she smiled. Then she removed his hand from her breast. "Babies don't wait," she said. "Loving does."

He laughed and headed for the shower. Before he left the villa, she was sound asleep again.

When he returned, he slipped quickly out of his clothes and slid into bed beside her. He didn't mean to awaken her, but she opened her eyes and smiled. "Again" was all she said, and this time their mating was as wild and as passionate as the sea in a storm.

Afterward she said, "Am I getting the hang of it?"

"You're doing fine," he said. "Although, as they say, practice makes perfect." He was just moving his hand upward along the inside of her thigh when the telephone rang again.

"Damn!" he exclaimed before he answered it. As he listened to the caller, his eyebrows lifted. "For you," he said, handing her the receiver.

"Maura, I thought you should know. Mrs. Matthews has started her labor. It's two weeks short of her due date." It was Golden; Maura had left a message for her so that Golden would know where to find her in case of an emergency.

"I'll be at her house in twenty minutes," Maura told her assistant.

Xan's hand remained on Maura's thigh, gently squeezing.

"I need to get to the Matthews's house as quickly as possible," she told Xan, sitting up in bed. "I have a feeling that it's going to be a long labor." The sheet fell away from her breasts, still tender and sensitive from their long session of lovemaking.

"And you have to be there to hold Mrs. Matthews's hand," he said, taking his own hand away.

This was something that he of all people understood. Just as she had understood when he had left to deliver Mrs. Jameson's baby.

She looked at him, sharing that understanding, and then suddenly her expression changed from tender to one so comical that he almost laughed.

"What," she said, "am I going to wear?"

"Since all our clothes have probably washed halfway to the Canary Islands with the tide, that's a good question."

"I have some clothes in my van," said Maura. "I keep them there for times when I'm officiating at long or difficult birthings. But I can hardly go outside like this."

Xan looked her nude body over judiciously, taking in her tawny smooth skin, her flowing hair coppery in the early-morning sunbeams slanting through the window blinds. "You'd certainly add your own brand of exoticism to the neighborhood. Old Frank Burney would probably find a number of plants to water in his yard, and as for Mrs. Burney, she'd think the worst of me. Which she already does, I'm afraid."

"She knows you, uh, entertain women here, I suppose."

Something flared in Xan's eyes, and he pulled her to him so fiercely that she almost cried out in alarm. "No," he said, his voice grating against her ear, "there have been no other women in this house since the day I met you. Nor will there be."

His embrace fairly crushed the breath out of her, and his kiss was searing and totally convincing. "Do you believe me?" he asked her. "Do you?"

She nodded, and the intent expression left his face. Reluctantly his hands fell away from her and he stepped down from the bed via the footstool with its needlepoint treads bearing the Copeland family crest. His naked body as he stood momentarily before her was beautiful to her, even more so now that she knew every inch of it intimately.

"I'll get your clothes," he said, and then he pulled on a pair of shorts and hurried from the room. Lying back against the soft pillows in the high four-poster bed, she smiled as she heard him singing on his way down the stairs.

"YOU KNOW," she said later, as she was dressing, "you could come with me to Ginny's."

Xan had just stepped from the shower and, a towel wrapped around his lean hips, was drying his hair with a blow dryer. He stopped the dryer and in the sudden stillness looked at her carefully, measuring her sincerity.

"Do you want me to?" he said.

"If you'd like," she said, her look level. Both of them were thinking of the fiasco when she'd observed him in the delivery room at Quinby. And both of them knew that more rode on his decision than on the birthing of Ginny Matthews's baby.

He thought for a moment; then he said quietly, "I'd like to go with you." After last night, he wanted to be with her.

They drove up to the Matthews's house in Maura's van. Ginny's husband met them on the front porch. "Xan, this is Joe Matthews," Maura said. The two men shook hands. They all moved into the house, a white clapboard bungalow flanked by carefully tended beds of nasturtiums. Xan was surprised to find that Ginny Matthews was up and moving around. From a tape player in the living room wafted gentle music, something by Brahms.

Maura took time to spend with Ginny, palpating her abdomen, taking her blood pressure, checking the fetal heart rate before preparing the bedroom where the baby would be born. "You'll know instinctively when to move around, when to be still," she told Ginny. "Let yourself flow with the experience. A relaxed body and mind are the best way to an easy labor." Then, tranquilly humming along with the music, Maura busied herself with preparations.

Joe remained with Ginny, massaging her back or feet when she requested it, sitting beside her on the bed when her labor deepened. The couple's two other children wandered in and out, very much a part of the proceedings, very interested in the progress of the birth of their new brother or sister. There was a lot of laughing and joking between Ginny and Joe, a camaraderie that reached out to include Xan and Maura in their family's joy. And through it all there was Maura, encouraging, lending her vital energy, reacting with concern and love to her patient's needs.

Maura found herself renewed and refreshed after the night with Xan, and she felt so filled with love that she could feel the healing energy of that emotion as she guided Ginny and Joe and their family toward the big moment. When the baby was born, she encouraged Joe to catch his new daughter, her eyes meeting Xan's at that special moment, and she felt herself fusing with him in a spirit of love and happiness that shook both of them to their souls.

Xan felt it, too. And his only thought was *I never knew it could be like this.* He was well aware that he was thinking not only of his love for Maura but of his own enlightenment about childbirth, which had never seemed so beautiful to him as when Maura conducted a birthing. The emotional flow, the insight and above all the peace he shared with Maura in that moment of birth combined in a revelatory moment that Xan Copeland would never forget.

Chapter Eleven

There had not only been rooms in her house to be filled, but also rooms in her heart. Maura hadn't realized before how empty she'd felt. And now that emptiness was filled with so much warmth and happiness that Maura could not imagine how she had ever been able to get along without Xan's love.

In the convent, the emphasis had been on God's love. But in her outreach midwifery practice, Maura had become accustomed to giving and receiving love from many kinds of people outside the order. That love gave her strength when it became clear to her that she must leave the convent. But it hadn't prepared her for the totality of her love for Xan Copeland, a love that permeated her whole life and her whole being.

Kathleen had been stunned by the news that Maura was in love with Xan Copeland. "You're not!" she said, her eyes widening at the thought. "You can't be in love with him. Didn't I warn you? Didn't I tell you that—"

"Wait a minute, Kathleen," Maura said impatiently. "It's different with Xan and me. He loves me. Really."

"Other women thought he loved them, too," said Kathleen darkly.

"Since Xan's fiancée broke their engagement, his practice has been his life," Maura said. "He hasn't had time for women."

"Well, then, how do you fit into his life? How does he fit into yours? You have different views about childbirth, and you both put your practice before everything else." Kathleen's eyes were worried.

Maura's thoughts flew to the moment when Ginny Matthews's baby was born. She could only hope that somehow, some way, she and Xan could integrate their lives and their beliefs. She loved Xan Copeland, and she wanted to be with him as much as possible. She had no doubt that he felt the same way.

"Anyway," she continued, "I'm going for an interview with Dr. Raymond Lyles, Quinby Hospital's chief of staff, sometime this week." Quickly she filled Kathleen in on the birthing-room concept.

Kathleen was excited by the news that such a facility might soon be available at Quinby. "I know a lot of young married women here on Teoway," Kathleen told her. "Lots of them have babies. If they want to use a birthing room, they have to go all the way to Charleston. You can imagine how worried they get as their due date approaches, thinking that they might not be able to make the twenty-mile drive to Charleston in time for the baby's arrival!"

"Why don't they look into home births? I'd be glad to show them my slides. You know I'm willing to serve any women who want a home birth, not just the Shuffletown women."

"No, Maura," Kathleen said gently. "Can't you see that they think it would be even worse if they counted on a home birth and then at the last minute had to be transported the twenty miles to Charleston anyway? Home births will become popular on Teoway Island only when you have local medical backup at Quinby Hospital."

More than she would have admitted to anyone, Maura was troubled about working in a hospital, but she was determined to go through with her discussion with Raymond Lyles for Xan's sake and for the sake of their relationship. It was the least she could do, especially when Xan seemed to be making an effort to modify his stance on childbirth. However, when she called Dr. Lyles's office at the hospital to make an appointment, his secretary said that Dr. Lyles was out of town for the day, but that he would call her when he returned.

Except that it wasn't Dr. Lyles who called her about the appointment the next day. It was Xan. Sounding jubilant, he said, "Can you come over to the hospital? Raymond is back, and he's ready to see you to talk about the birthing room at Quinby Hospital."

As always, Maura's heart lightened at the sound of Xan's voice. She longed to see him; their separate schedules hadn't allowed them to be together in days. But the time was inconvenient for her, as much as she wanted to be with Xan and do what he asked of her.

She'd just pulled on a leotard and tights. "I'm getting ready to teach an exercise class," she said reluctantly. "Must it be now?"

"As soon as possible. Can't Golden take over your exercise class?" Xan's words were impatient.

"Well—" Somehow she was feeling pushed into this.

"Maura, Raymond seems extremely enthusiastic. He visited a small hospital up in Yewville that recently began offering family-centered maternity care, and he liked what he saw."

She made herself think. Xan sounded so excited about it all, as though he really believed in the birthing room and what it could provide. Maybe there was, after all, some way they could come to a meeting of the minds.

"I can be there in about half an hour," she told him, rapidly figuring in her head how long it would take her to run a brush through her hair and find something suitable to wear.

"I'll meet you in the main lobby of the hospital," he told her. "And, Maura, I can't help but think that this is going to be a good thing."

Maura didn't share Xan's confidence, but she hung up and explained the situation to Golden, who was willing to take over the exercise class for Maura, and then she hurried to her closet, where she found a pale-green linen dress that looked businesslike enough for this meeting. As she dressed, she realized how apprehensive she was about meeting this Dr. Lyles when she fumbled with the back zipper and dropped one of her simple pearl earrings so that it skidded across the hardwood floor.

She was just scrambling to her feet after retrieving the earring when Golden appeared in the doorway to her room. "You look pretty," she observed, taking in the pale-green linen and the earrings.

"Thanks," said Maura. "I just wish I felt—well, more up to this." She finally managed to affix the earring to her right earlobe, where it felt anything but comfortable.

Golden leaned against the door, regarding Maura with curiosity. "Why are you going to see Dr. Lyles, anyway? I thought you didn't want to conduct hospital births?"

Maura walked to the window and looked out at the wide cotton field reaching to the horizon, biting her lip as she always did when she was in doubt about something. "It's only a chance to be a labor coach in his birthing room. I really don't want to be merely a labor coach for someone else's patients, as I'm sure you know. That's what I was doing before I began my practice as a midwife conducting home births."

"You still haven't answered my question," probed Golden carefully. "Why, then, are you going to see Dr. Lyles about being a labor coach at his hospital?"

"I think I owe it to my patients," she said honestly. "They deserve to be able to go to Quinby for emergency care. And if this is the means to that end..." and her voice trailed off in uncertainty.

"Well," said Golden doubtfully, "good luck." As the sound of female voices drifted upstairs, they realized that women were beginning to arrive for their exercise class. Golden started to leave, then stopped and peered around the edge of the doorway. "Are you sure," Golden said knowingly, not fooled a bit, "that you aren't about to give up everything you've worked for just so you can spend a little more time with Xan Copeland?"

Maura whipped her head around, ready to answer, and her right earring went flying across the room. She stooped to look for it, feeling overwhelmingly flustered. When at last she found the earring, Golden's footsteps were retreating down the stairs. Her heart pounding, Maura clutched her earring in her fist, relieved that she hadn't had to answer Golden's incisive question.

At the hospital, Xan greeted her warmly with a kiss on the cheek. "You look as cool as a cucumber," he told her, seemingly delighted with her appearance.

"I feel like I'm going to be handling a hot potato," she confessed. She took his arm. "Tell me what Dr. Lyles has said about this birthing-room concept."

"He's raring to go on the whole idea," Xan said as they strolled down the corridor to Raymond Lyles's office. "I'll let him tell you about it himself." He knocked on Dr. Lyles's office door, and a gravelly voice called out, "Come in, come in."

Maura stood uncertainly in the doorway until Xan grasped her elbow reassuringly and urged her forward. She held out her hand to Raymond Lyles, and he stood and gripped it. His handclasp was strong and sure, and he stared at her piercingly from beneath thick gray eyebrows for a moment. Then he spared her an almost imperceptible nod and invited her to sit on the brown leather chair across from his desk.

"I've told Maura about your idea for a birthing room," said Xan, sitting on the chair next to hers.

Dr. Lyles drew a folder from a drawer in his desk. "Xan tells me you've had experience as a labor coach in such rooms."

A quick glance in Xan's direction showed him to be smiling at her encouragingly. She cleared her throat. "I have," she said.

"Here at Quinby," said Dr. Lyles, "I've always preferred the traditional birth methods. The mother goes immediately to the labor room when she arrives at the hospital, then is moved to the delivery room for the delivery of her baby. Then the baby is taken to the nursery and the mother is finally assigned to a hospital room in the maternity ward."

Maura nodded. She had known all of this, and she wished that Dr. Lyles would get to the point.

"With a birthing room, the mother would labor, deliver and recover in the same room. Her husband would be present for the delivery if he preferred, and the baby would be allowed in the room with the mother whenever she liked."

Maura thought of the heart-wrenching look on Sandra Giles's face when she saw her baby girl carted off to the hospital nursery immediately after delivery. The memory of that look gave her the determination to listen to Raymond Lyles, and if necessary to encourage him to go ahead with what was for him a revolutionary new idea in childbirth procedures. But as she listened, it seemed to Maura that Dr. Lyles's birthing room concept didn't go far enough. She knew that flowered sheets on a birthing bed and a midwife coach for labor could not approximate the comfort and reassurance of being with one's own family at such a stressful time as birth.

"I'd like to see you go a step further," Maura said earnestly. "True family-centered care would involve allowing children to be present for the birth of their new brothers and sisters. At the parents' discretion, of course." She was thinking of Ginny and Joe Matthews's warm and happy experience.

Xan stared at her. Clearly he hadn't expected her to say anything of the sort.

Raymond Lyles drew himself up, all bluster. "I don't think we're ready for that at Quinby," he said. He lowered those grizzled eyebrows at her. "I don't think parents are ready for it, either. So tell me, are you interested in being my labor coach or not?"

Unprepared for the sudden question, Maura blinked.

"Well, are you? You wanted access to my delivery room. Surely you're not going to balk at coaching labor in my birthing room."

Everything, Maura could see, at Quinby Hospital was referred to by Raymond Lyles as "mine." Looking at him across the broad shiny expanse of his big desk, his eyes piercing her with their challenge, she was reminded of other eyes in another place far away.

The expression in this man's eyes was one of total authority, and the expression in those other eyes had been, too. Dr. Lyles reminded her of the mother superior—a painful memory, to say the least.

Something snapped within her. Maura gripped the arms of her chair so hard that her knuckles turned white. Xan noticed, but he didn't understand.

"Maura," said Xan quickly, seeing that he would have to intercede. "Why don't you give it a try?"

Suddenly Maura stood up. "I'll think about it," she said, her voice low and troubled. "Dr. Lyles, I'll need time."

"How long?" he shot back.

"At—at least a week."

"As long as that? I want to get on with this!" The redoubtable Dr. Lyles was annoyed.

Xan looked from one to the other. He didn't understand Maura. His hopes, which he had built up so high, began to tumble one by one.

Dr. Lyles pressed his lips tightly together. "One week. Be back here next Monday to let me know. Ten o'clock in the morning."

Maura nodded. She flicked a look at Xan, an unreadable look. Then she bolted for the door.

Xan took off after her. He caught up with her in the hospital lobby. "Maura, are you crazy? You should have grabbed at the opportunity to work in his birthing room. Don't you know that he might get someone else?"

Curious glances toward the two of them convinced Maura that they should remove this discussion elsewhere. "Come outside. I don't want to talk in here."

Xan followed her to the door, but as they reached it, the PA system announced, "Dr. Copeland. Dr. Alexander Copeland, report to the delivery room at once."

"I can't talk to you now, I'm being paged. Listen, Maura, I just don't understand you. First you want time because you don't know if you're ready for a relationship with me. Then I think it's all settled, and now you want time to think over being a labor coach in the new birthing room. What is it with you? Why do you always need time?" Xan looked totally frustrated.

"There are all these—these hospital rules I'd have to follow. You still haven't told me whether or not you'll be my supervising physician. And I don't *want* to be a labor coach," she said tightly.

"What you want and what it's realistic to want are two different things," he retorted angrily. Two frail elderly ladies dodged around them, and they had to move. Again the impersonal nasal clatter of the PA system broke in: "Dr. Copeland, please report to the delivery room. Dr. Alexander Copeland..."

"Maura, you wouldn't have to give up your private practice, you know. This birthing-room labor coaching would only be part-time for those of my patients who request it. Why didn't you say yes?" Xan wanted to know.

"Dr. Lyles is so—so patriarchal," she said. "I'd have to knuckle under to him."

"That's the way it is," said Xan. "He's from the old school. At Quinby Hospital, he's the ultimate authority."

"If I worked in his birthing room, I'd have to submit to his authority. I don't want to do that." Maura's jaw was set in a stubborn line.

"You've worked in the medical profession for a long time. You understand how it works. Quinby Hospital is no exception," argued Xan. He had learned to gauge Maura's reactions by assessing her facial expressions; her anguished expression told him that her emotions were in a turmoil, much more of a turmoil than the situation warranted. Why didn't she trust him enough to talk to him, damn it! He'd been as understanding as any man could be. He'd asked all he could; he'd probed deeper than he felt he had a right to probe. What more could he possibly do to make her trust him?

She looked up at him, pleading for understanding. "The way it is now, with my working at home births, I don't have to worry about submitting to anyone else's authority. I conduct birthings the way I see fit, according to my own intuition and skill. I'd feel constrained in a birthing room."

"Aren't you forgetting that it would be a chance for us to work together?"

Maura cringed inwardly at the ice in Xan's tone. "I'm not forgetting that at all." She lifted her chin a trifle, refusing to be manipulated into the decision Xan wanted her to make.

Xan felt totally exasperated. Weeks ago, when he'd first found out that Maura was a midwife, he had despaired that he would ever be able to incorporate her into his life. Now, when everything at last seemed to be on the right track, she was balking.

"You don't understand," Maura began.

"I think I do," said Xan, his eyes glittering with anger. "Every hospital has rules, and I can't imagine why something like a few rules would be so important to you. You just don't want us to work together. And you're unwilling to give up your high-flying ideas about childbirth to stoop to working at Quinby Hospital."

"But—"

"I've done the best I can do to make it possible for us to work together, if only in a limited way, and you refuse to take even the smallest step toward that goal. You may have alienated Raymond Lyles to the point where he'll no longer consider your working here. As far as I'm concerned, Maura, you can take all your childbirth philosophies back to that farmhouse of yours and think about them until hell freezes over. There's no point in our discussing it further, now or ever." He bit off the words sharply, his chest heaving. Maura longed to reach out her hand and touch him gently on the cheek, but his forbidding expression precluded any display of affection.

"Dr. Copeland, Dr. Alexander Copeland," ground the PA system monotonously.

With a last look of total fury, Xan clamped his lips together and strode purposefully away, disappearing between a set of swinging doors at the end of the corridor and leaving Maura standing there with tears welling up in her eyes.

"Excuse me, miss," said a boy trying to maneuver a trolley of flowers past the heavy glass doors, and

Maura turned and ran blindly from the lobby out into the warm summer afternoon.

Xan was right. She was always asking for time. It was because she always felt rushed pell-mell, rushed into things that other people took for granted as part of their lives. How could she explain? It was time to tell him everything, all about the convent and the rules she couldn't accept there and her clash with authority; her past was a part of her present, but she hadn't been willing to admit it until now.

She had thought she had come so far. Indeed, she had come a long way, but clearly not far enough. If she loved Xan, she should be able to open every part of her life to him. Now she knew that she should have told Xan the whole story, should have told him she was an ex-nun and all the ramifications it had in her life. But what if she had waited too long? The pit of her stomach felt heavy, leaden. She had planned to tell him in her own good time. That time had never arrived. Now it might never arrive.

For Maura, this opportunity to coach labor in Quinby Hospital's new birthing room was shaping up into a personal crisis of the highest magnitude. Xan thought he knew what the issue was, but he really didn't.

Oh, Xan, Xan, she cried silently, tears streaming down her face as she stumbled toward the parking lot. *What if I can never make you understand?*

Chapter Twelve

"But, Maura, why don't you just tell Dr. Lyles that I'll be the labor coach in his birthing room? I'd like to, really I would." Golden's hazel eyes were earnest beneath the ragged old straw hat she wore to protect her from the hot Carolina sun.

Maura stopped spading the rich black earth and wiped the perspiration from her brow with her handkerchief. Golden had been taking on more and more responsibility within the practice lately. The good sense of Golden's suggestion almost bowled her over. "I never thought of it," she admitted ruefully. "I was so overwhelmed with my own concerns, my own problems. Of course," she said briskly, returning her attention to the row of herbs, "I'll suggest you, Golden. It'll give you additional experience in labor coaching, and it will provide Dr. Lyles with his mid-wife coach."

"My presence will also leave the way open for further negotiations for the McNeill Birth Center to use Quinby Hospital for emergency backup care. Let's not forget that important angle." Golden smiled as she pulled off her gardening gloves and gazed at the herb garden with satisfaction. "The sage is coming along real fine, isn't is, Maura?"

"I'm pleased with it," said Maura.

"In fact the only thing you're not pleased with is Xan Copeland," said Golden. "Don't think I haven't noticed you mooning around here. He hasn't called all week. Is something wrong?"

"Everything," said Maura emphatically, turning over a huge shovelful of dirt, "is wrong. It's so wrong it doesn't bear talking about. So please don't ask questions."

"I thought everything was fine between the two of you. In fact I expected to see the sign out front changed to read: McNEILL AND COPELAND BIRTH CENTER. You know, the two of you would be an unbeatable combination. Hospital births or home births, you pays your money and you takes your choice."

Golden's attempt at levity was lost on Maura, who attacked the ground even more viciously with her shovel. The shovel met with a stubborn resistance, and so Maura fell on her knees and scooped the dirt aside until a big rock was revealed. She tugged at the rock until her face grew red from the exertion, finally falling back panting, not having budged the rock one inch. She had, however, mangled a fingernail. Frustrated tears sprang to her eyes, and Golden knew better than to think that the frustration was caused by the immovability of the rock. The immovability of Xan Copeland was what had caused Maura's tears.

Golden sank down on her knees beside Maura. "Hey, I'm sorry if I said something I shouldn't have said." She paused. "I think you need to get out and do something instead of sitting around here. How about driving into Charleston with me tonight? We could take in a movie. Want to?"

Maura wiped a tear from her cheek, leaving a black smudge. "Kathleen and Don have invited me out to dinner. I've already told them I'd go. But thank you, Golden. Maybe some other time, okay?" She smiled a watery smile.

"Okay. I'll put these gardening tools away." Golden hoisted the shovel and the hoe, heading for the toolshed.

Maura slowly rose to her feet, brushing the dust from her clothes. This day was typical of her days lately. Deep depression, unchanged by any of the experiences that usually brought her pleasure. The black cloud of gloom that had descended on her when Xan had walked through those doors at the hospital and out of her life would not be vanquished. Even an especially joyous birthing this week, to parents who had thought they would never be able to have a baby of their own, had not done anything to dispel her lassitude of spirit. Nothing, it seemed, would give her comfort except Xan.

But Xan had not called, nor had he visited her, nor had he expressed any desire to do so. He had simply left her life, dropped out of it. Even after all they had become to each other, she was nothing more to him than his other women. Useful to him for a while, then when he didn't want her anymore, whoosh, she was out of his life, just like that. She had thought that their relationship was special. Well, that just proved she didn't know how to handle the real world yet. Kathleen had been right all along.

Which is what Kathleen tried to avoid saying when she and Don stopped by the farmhouse to pick Maura up for dinner that night. It had been Kathleen's idea that they all go out together; they had seen little of each other as a threesome ever since Maura had moved out of the Teoway Island house. Kathleen had visited Maura in the middle of the week and noticed how pale Maura looked, how tired. Maura had poured out the story of what had happened with Xan, and the hurt in her brown eyes had torn at Kathleen's heart.

Now Kathleen sent Don out to look at Maura's herb garden and while he was gone, she spoke bluntly to her sister as they stood at the kitchen door. "Xan hasn't called?"

Wearily Maura shook her head.

"What will you do now?" asked Kathleen, worried about the despair on Maura's face.

"I don't know. I really love him, Kathleen." But her voice was dispirited, sad.

"You love him. Oh, Maura." Kathleen's words fell between them, heavy as stones.

"You warned me. Maybe you were right. But he said he loved"—here her voice broke—"loved me." She finished the sentence painfully, her heart breaking.

"And you honestly believed that he loved you?"

Maura nodded. "There wasn't any doubt in my mind."

"Does he know why you don't want to work in a hospital again?" Kathleen's question was pointed and direct.

Maura shook her head. "I—I've never been able to tell him," she said helplessly.

Their private conversation was interrupted by Don, who stamped his feet loudly on the back porch to shake the garden dirt off and said, "That's one fine garden you've got, Maura." The pregnant cat, lately christened Mehitabel, lumbered heavily off the porch, out of Don's way.

Kathleen propelled them toward the car, exchanging a look with Maura that said they'd keep their conversation private.

"Where are you taking us to dinner?" asked Kathleen idly once they were on the road in Don's Mercedes sedan. Maura, sitting alone in the back seat, had assumed that they would be driving into Charleston to eat at one of the many fine restaurants there.

"We're going to drive down the coast to a little restaurant called the Shrimpboat," Don said. "It's just a tiny place, sort of a local secret. The food is supposed to be wonderful."

In the back seat, Maura felt a white-hot pain sear the region around her heart. Of course Don couldn't know the significance of that particular restaurant in her life, and she couldn't seem to summon the effort it would take to ask him if they could go someplace else. How could she bear to sit in that same restaurant where she had blurted out that she loved Xan? How could she look out at the view of the shrimp trawlers and the docks and not think about that night, that wonderful night, when their love had become a reality?

Blinking back the tears that clouded her vision, she stared out the window at the passing panorama of green countryside, of great moss-draped trees overhanging the road, seeing none of it. All she could see was Xan's smiling face, his laughing eyes, that funny bump in the middle of his nose. All she could think about was loving him, even now.

Much too soon they reached the restaurant, and as she followed Kathleen to their table she kept her eyes riveted on her sister's shining hair. She didn't want to look out the big window at the cove, didn't want to see any of it. The pain inside her cut to the core of her very soul.

Blindly, only going through the paces, oblivious to the curious way Don was looking at her, untouched by Kathleen's quiet concern, she stared at the menu, not knowing what to order. Finally she let Don order something, anything, she didn't know what. And after they had placed their order, she heard Kathleen say apprehensively, as though from very far away, "Oh, Maura, I'm afraid he's here. Xan Copeland."

And then, incredulously, she swiveled her head toward the window, toward the very table where the two of them had sat such a short time ago, such a long time ago, and her eyes locked with the deep-green eyes of the man she'd thought had loved her, and they went through her like the thrust of a very hard, very cold sword.

The woman with him was blond and svelte and dainty, a petite thing with the look of money about her clothes and shoes and jewelry. She didn't see the exchange between Xan and Maura; she was admiring the view from the window. Just as Maura had admired it when Xan had brought her here.

How could he have brought someone else here, to their special place? How *could* he? Maura struggled through the meal in a fog of agony, the food tasteless in her mouth. Kathleen and Don tried to distract her, and they were very kind. But all Maura could think about was Xan being with someone else. After they had eaten, it was with immense relief that Maura stumbled from the restaurant, holding her head self-consciously higher than usual and avoiding looking in the direction of Xan and his date.

"Maura," said Kathleen suddenly as they drove home, "come home with us for the night." She turned in the seat, her anxious face illuminated by the lights of the car behind them. "You could go to mass with us in the morning in the little Teoway Island church. Would you like that?"

Maura smiled bleakly. "Really, I can go home. I'm going to survive the breakup with Xan, you know." Although at the moment she wasn't sure of the truth of that statement.

"We wouldn't even have to stop by the farm-house," Kathleen told her. "I'll let you borrow some of my clothes tomorrow. And anyway, you said that

Golden is on call all weekend. Oh, please come home with us. I'd really like you to."

It was kind of Kathleen, and Maura really didn't want to go home alone to the big, dark house.

She sighed. "Okay. I'd like that."

"Good," said Don. "You can keep Kathleen company tomorrow after church. I have a tennis date."

And so it was that Maura drove back to Teoway Island with Kathleen and Don instead of to her farmhouse, a circumstance that Xan Copeland hadn't counted on.

DAMN, HE THOUGHT to himself as he drove up in front of the McNeill Birth Center. All the lights in the house were out, and the countryside itself was dark in this remote area. He had hoped Maura would still be awake.

He'd rushed his date through her dinner, had made up some sort of story so that he could drive her back to Charleston right afterward. She'd taken it all pretty well, considering. Then he'd driven at breakneck speed back to the farmhouse, knowing he had to see Maura.

He got out of his car and slammed the door, hard, thinking the noise might rouse her. But the only sound was the chirp of crickets in the underbrush and the high, clear cry of a night bird. He strode beneath the pecan trees, heard the rustling of their leaves above him as the wind blew gently through the branches.

He'd hated it that she'd been at the Shrimpboat,

that their eyes had met so impersonally. She'd looked crushed, hurt. He didn't blame her. He would have felt the same way in her place. He'd only taken his date there in a futile attempt to forget Maura. So now he had to tell Maura this, had to talk to her, he had to.

He knocked on the door. No answer. Impatiently he knocked again. Still no answer. The place was quiet, too quiet. She'd be used to people knocking in the middle of the night, coming to get her for imminent birthings.

He bounded off the porch and ran around to the back like a man demented. He banged on the door as hard as he could. "Maura!" he yelled in frustration, backing off the porch and looking up at the window to her bedroom. He bent down and picked up a handful of gravel from the path. He tossed it against her window, but no surprised face appeared behind the glass, no hand lifted the heavy shade.

Still not ready to abandon all hope, he ran around the front again and used his fists to make a racket against the front door that would have awakened anyone but the dead. No one answered. She really wasn't there.

His shoulders slumped in disappointment. He wondered where she was. She could be anywhere; she birthed babies all over Shuffletown. She might be gone for hours.

He sat down in the hammock, fighting his regret and the pain that went with it. How he longed to hold her in his arms and make everything right between them! Ever since he'd walked away from her in the hospital he'd regretted it. He'd spoken too hastily, and then his pride wouldn't let him go to her. He wanted her to come to him. But now he'd had enough of his own pride, had almost choked on it. He clenched his fists, overwhelmed with his longing for her. And then he heard the plaintive meow.

His eyes pierced the gloom, searching for Mehitabel. Another meow, and he saw her. She was lying in an empty box that had been tossed on the porch. He looked closer, his eyes widening. Then he knelt, scratching the cat behind the ear. He was rewarded by an answering purr.

He smiled and shook his head. Then he sat down beside the box. Maura was always talking about cherishing life's beginnings, and knowing how nurturing her spirit was, he presumed her philosophy extended to cats, too.

"Well, Mehitabel, old girl," he said conversationally, "it looks like we're in for a long night. Why did you pick tonight of all nights to have your kittens?"

MAURA, ENSCONCED IN THE BIG BED at Kathleen's house, slept fitfully. They'd decided the night before to get up around ten o'clock and go to the eleven o'clock mass at the small and rustic Teoway Island church. After mass, when Don had left for his tennis date, she and Kathleen sat on the long deck overlooking the Teoway Island marshes. A belted kingfisher dived for fish amid the tall reeds, distracting them as they ate the lunch Kathleen had prepared, chicken sandwiches embellished with watercress and accompanied by tall glasses of iced tea. Rather, Kathleen ate. Maura only shoved her sandwich around on her plate and stared into space.

"What am I going to do, Kath?" asked Maura finally.

"Now you're asking me? When it may be too late to do anything?"

"She was pretty, wasn't she?" said Maura in utter discouragement, thinking of the woman who had been with Xan in the restaurant.

"You're prettier," said Kathleen firmly.

"But he's not embroiled in conflict with her," said Maura unhappily. "If we only didn't have the child-birth thing at issue, everything would have been all right between us."

This was supposed to be a light lunch and a sisterly chat. Only it had become more than a chat. This could only be classified under the heading of a full-fledged discussion. Kathleen stood and paced the deck, thinking.

She turned back to Maura. "I think you're going to have to talk to Xan," she said.

"If he wanted to talk to me, he'd have called," said Maura stonily.

Kathleen knelt at her sister's side, gazing up at her earnestly. "You know how I worried about you when you first started going out with Xan? How I feared that you didn't have the experience to handle him? And how self-assured you were, telling me that you could take care of yourself?"

"Naive, that's what I was," replied Maura with a

trace of bitterness. Then she burst out, "Oh, Kathleen, I'm afraid I've ruined everything!" Kathleen was startled to see Maura's brown eyes swimming with tears.

"All right, you were naive. But naive doesn't mean stupid. If you love him, go after him. You have a lot of things to tell Xan, things you should have told him long ago. Tell him, Maura. Tell him now."

"You make it sound easy," said Maura.

"It isn't easy. Sharing your emotional life with another person never is. You've experienced heavy emotions vicariously, through your patients. But actually putting yourself on the line emotionally, trusting another person so totally that your whole life is open to him—that's one of the things you never learned to do. But if you care about Xan, you're going to have to learn."

"I could call his answering service," said Maura. "They always know where he is."

"Then call. This isn't the time to be stubborn. Do it now, before you lose heart."

Maura rose from her chair with a rueful smile. "Thanks for the sisterly advice," she said.

Kathleen stood up, feeling as though she, not Maura, were the elder sister. "Don't thank me yet," she warned as Maura stepped inside the house to telephone. "Wait and see if it works."

XAN URGED HIS HONDA along the rutted road, getting a kind of grim satisfaction out of the jouncing ride. Keeping the motorcycle from running up the trunk of one of the numerous pine trees in this area was a difficult job; come to think of it, he wasn't exactly sure he didn't want to. A collision with a tree seemed at this point a prospect a lot less agonizing than the inner pain he was feeling.

He'd watched Mehitabel give birth to four tiny kittens there on Maura's side porch. He sat and offered encouragement to the laboring cat until dawn peeped over the horizon, knowing that Maura wouldn't have wanted the cat to be alone at such a time. All the while he'd expected Maura to arrive home, tired yet exalted in that radiant way of hers, when he would gather her in his arms and tell her how much he loved her.

Finally, after the sun had fully risen, turning the dewdrops on the roses into diamonds, he rose, too. He left his cramped position beside the cat's box and stretched, admitting to himself that Maura wasn't coming home any time soon. He was tired himself, didn't know if he could keep his eyes open all the way back to his villa. But he did, and he'd fallen into bed exhausted to catch a few hours of sleep before he'd awakened and the sadness settled over him again.

The winding road led to one of his favorite places on Teoway Island, a place where he often went to find inner peace. He'd go there now and give himself over to it. He already knew what he'd done wrong. He hadn't fully accounted for the sadness in her, and he'd asked too much. And in some ways he hadn't asked enough. About her past, for instance. He'd have to clear up the mystery about that before they could pick up and go on. They could still have a satis-

fying life together. It was up to him to figure out
where all the pieces fit, that's all.

MAURA SWUNG ALONG the hard-packed sand, placing
one foot in front of the other with great concentration. She had to concentrate on something as simple
as walking in order not to think about what she was
about to do.

She'd called Xan's service, and the operator — the
gabby one, thank goodness — had asked her if she
wanted to page him on his electronic beeper. Xan had,
she said, gone for a motorcycle ride to the Vrooman
mansion, an old plantation house on Teoway Island.

"No," Maura had told the operator quickly, it
wasn't necessary to page Xan. And then she'd borrowed a pair of white jeans and a saffron-colored Teoway Island T-shirt from Kathleen and set out for the
Vrooman mansion.

She knew the winding road Xan had ridden to the
Vrooman place. It snaked through a palmetto-oak-
magnolia maritime forest, and she wouldn't attempt a
walk through such wild terrain by herself. The other
way to reach the mansion was along the beach. Although it was a longer route, she didn't mind it because she had thought she'd welcome the chance to
think.

But now she didn't want to think at all. Confronting
Xan was something she'd do better to handle by
instinct, like birthing babies. She was an instinct-
oriented person, especially where human relationships were concerned.

Now she could see the tall ruins of the Vrooman mansion reared against the cloudless blue sky. Her heart leaped to her mouth. What if Xan wasn't there after all and she had wasted the trip?

She climbed to the top of the beach-front dune ridge and from the advantage of this height surveyed the mansion site. No sign of Xan. So she skidded down the side of the dune, her borrowed sneakers filling with sand, which was uncomfortable to say the least. She trudged on, peering ahead through the lush foliage. Was that bright-blue metal glinting there in the sunlight? Yes! It was Xan's Honda! She approached slowly, thumbs linked over the edges of her pockets, wondering where he might be.

The Vrooman mansion had been built in the 1780s and had withstood an earthquake, hurricanes and occupation by enemy troops in two wars. It had been the home of the Vrooman family, Dutch immigrants who had grown the valuable long-staple sea island cotton. The cotton had fallen prey to the boll weevil after World War I, and the house had stood vacant for fifty years.

"Xan?" she said, climbing up on the brick porch at the rear of the house. The warm fruity fragrance of magnolia blossoms in the forest blended with the richness of the odor of the surrounding marshland and rose somnolently to be wafted away by the tangy salt breeze from the ocean. It was quiet here, and private.

Maura peered through one of the windows. It had been boarded up once, but vandals had torn away the boards. The pane was dusty, so she rubbed it with the side of her hand and looked through the clean spot.

Someone looked back. "Xan!" she exclaimed. Their eyes met and held with a startling intensity. Without a word he whirled and came to the door, where he hesitated. He wanted to rush to her and enfold her in his arms, but something stopped him. The look in her eyes; it was not soft, but determined. His heart sank.

"I was looking for you," she said.

"You found me," he replied, and she couldn't detect a welcome in his voice. The words were just words.

"Interesting place," she said, stalling for time, striving for a semblance of normality.

He tried to match her tone. "I didn't know you wanted to see the Vrooman place or I'd have brought you here myself," he said.

She shook her head. "I didn't want to see the Vrooman mansion. I wanted to see you."

"So you said," he answered. "What's the momentous occasion?" He regretted the question immediately, wincing inwardly. It sounded much too cynical.

She shrugged. "I just want to talk," she said.

"Sit down here," he said, gesturing to an area of the great open porch. "Right on the brick. That's it. Smell the magnolias? They're in bloom now. That's one of the reasons I came here today." There, that sounded more friendly. He inhaled deeply.

The magnolias did smell wonderful. Maura inhaled, too, putting off saying anything. The sun was a welcome warmth on her face.

"Now what were we going to talk about?" he asked. It was his eyes she noticed most; the pupils were large and dark, the irises deeply green. He looked upon her with expectancy, waiting.

If only he knew how hard this was for her! Nuns were taught to wait passively, not to take the initiative. That kind of training was hard to overcome. "I'm not going to be a labor coach in the Quinby Hospital birthing room," she said firmly.

Despair clutched at Xan's stomach; she was leading with bad news. "I wish you were," he said quietly.

"I have to work the way I want to work. I'm going to continue with home births. I want you to know that first, before I tell you anything else."

"You mean there's more?" He stared at her. She looked beautiful, as always. But there was a courage about her, too, and a determination. He had always admired her determination.

Maura nodded. She had gone too far to stop now. "In California—" she began, but Xan interrupted.

"Look, Maura, I don't expect to hear about unhappy love affairs or—"

"Love affairs? After that night we spent at your villa, you think I've had love affairs?" She gaped at him, two red spots staining her cheeks.

"It has me puzzled, all right," he said ruefully. "I know I was the first man you ever slept with, but there must have been someone else, the way you clam up whenever the subject of California creeps into the conversation."

"All this time you've thought I had an ex-lover somewhere?"

"Until that night, yes, I did. Now I think—oh, hell, I don't know what I think."

She couldn't help it. She started to laugh, to laugh so hard that tears began to slide unheeded down her cheeks. Xan viewed her with alarm, wondering if she was hysterical, if he should offer her a handkerchief. Finally he did what his instincts told him to do: he reached out and pulled her into his arms, where she stopped laughing and sobbed and sobbed against his shirt, dampening it with tears. "Shh," he murmured, "it's all right. Whatever happened in California, it couldn't have been that bad."

She bit her lip and hiccuped, loving how strong his arms felt, how they provided such a safe haven. "It was horrible," she said. "At the time I thought it was the worst thing that could ever happen to me. Until lately, when I found out that the worst thing that could happen to me was to lose you. Oh, Xan, I've missed you so!"

He kissed her eyes, and when he looked down at her it was to admire the delicate tracery of veins on the lids. Maura: how much he loved her! "Tell me," he said unsteadily. "Tell me everything."

And so she settled down in his arms, his heartbeat steadying her, and she poured out the story. She was all right until she got to the part about the mother superior ordering her to stop her outreach practice. How well she remembered it! Her voice quavered as she told Xan how she had pleaded to continue.

She'd sat before the mother superior, hands folded demurely in her lap, but underneath her quiet facade her emotions were seething. Finally she'd lost her cool. "But Rosa Vaccaro is in labor right this very minute, her husband has sent for me, I must go," she had babbled. With the stern mother superior staring her down, she couldn't really believe that it was all over, the practice she had built up from nothing. What would these people do? Rosa had never been in a hospital in her life, was scared of hospitals, couldn't afford one. What would happen to women like Rosa?

The mother superior was steadfast. "You must telephone Mrs. Vaccaro and tell her to call an ambulance to bring her to the hospital. We cannot guarantee your safety on the streets of this neighborhood any longer. We will not allow the same thing that happened to Sister Angela to happen to you."

"Mother, please listen," began Maura, ready to plead, to bargain, to do anything. Her place was with the poor people in their homes, doing the work she had been called to do. She had no fear for her own safety.

"No," said the mother superior. "When you came to us, you took solemn vows of chastity, poverty and obedience. *Obedience,* Sister Maura. Remember that vow." She dismissed Maura with a wave of her hand. "Now go."

Maura had gone. She had prayed, and she knew what she had to do. She could not submit to authority, not in this instance. Her work, the work she loved, was all-important. With deep regret and many a backward glance, she left the convent. In so doing, she was

refused hospital privileges at the hospital the convent
served. And knowing that she could not remain in
that neighborhood where the looming presence of the
hospital and the convent would continue to remind
her of that awful heartbreaking conflict, she had fled
to Shuffletown, where the people were also poor and
had need of her services.

She could be dedicated to the service of people who
needed her, even outside the convent. But even in
her wildest dreams she had not foreseen the complication of meeting Dr. Alexander Copeland.

"YOU'RE AN EX-*NUN*?" Xan said incredulously when
she had finished.

She nodded solemnly.

"There was no other man," he said, as if to con-
vince himself.

"No," she assured him.

"I thought—oh, my God. I thought you were thinking of someone else those times that you wouldn't let
me—" He stared at her. "I was trying to make love to
an ex-nun."

She nodded again. "I didn't want you to know. I
couldn't talk about it, the subject was so painful. Can
you imagine how terrible it was for me to leave, Xan?
Giving up my dreams? Even my whole identity, the
way I thought of myself, was gone after I left the convent. It wasn't until I met you that I began to think of
myself as a woman for the first time, with a woman's
wants and needs."

Xan was very quiet. Then he pulled her into his

arms and held her tightly, as though he would never let her go.

"To work in a hospital," she said, her words muffled against his chest, "would remind me too much of what it was like in California after I had to discontinue my outreach practice."

"How? Surely Quinby Hospital is different from that place in California."

She shook her head. "I coached patients in labor at the hospital my convent served for several months after I was ordered to give up my outreach practice, until I made up my mind to leave. It was an intensely unhappy period of my life, longing to officiate at home birthings and knowing I might never be able to again. I decided then that I have a right to my privacy, and that my autonomy as a midwife should be respected. Maybe someday I'll be able to work in a hospital, but not yet. I just couldn't handle the absolute obeisance to Dr. Lyles."

"Now that you've told me these things, I won't ask you to work in Quinby's birthing room," said Xan. "If you'd told me before, I never would have asked you in the first place. I understand wanting to be your own person, believe me." And to Maura this hard-won understanding, at last, was a wonderful relief.

"I'm going to recommend Golden to Dr. Lyles when I see him tomorrow," she told him. "She really wants to work in the birthing room."

"Golden will do a fine job."

"So you won't be annoyed with me if I continue my home births?"

He leaned back and looked down at her. He shook his head. "I won't be annoyed at you, no matter what. I've seen you work. I've come to believe in you, and I admire what you do. I think I've been old-fashioned and stubborn and, well, I've been a fool. I'd like to be your sponsoring obstetrician. That is, if you still want me to be."

"You mean it? Really?"

"Really. I think I can get you delivery-room and emergency-room privileges at Quinby when and if you want them. Raymond Lyles will come around; he's already proved that he's ready to change childbirth procedures at Quinby by bringing in a birthing room. In fact I suggest that we institute some sort of merger so that our patients may choose any birth method that appeals to them. You've opened my eyes to all the possibilities, Maura."

"You mean you want to be part of McNeill Birth Center?"

Xan shook his head. "I'd like my office and your birth center to remain separate, but we'll refer patients to each other and consult with each other when necessary. We can let our patients make their own decisions; I know we can work it out if we try. You and me—the art of midwifery and the science of modern obstetrics blended. Would that suit you?"

"It sounds perfect," she said, amazed.

"You look so surprised," he told her.

"I am. Very."

"And I have another merger in mind also."

She looked at him questioningly, unsuspecting.

"Marry me, Maura. Soon."

It was too much to take in at once. "Marry you?" she said weakly.

He smiled down at her, a fond smile. "I want you to be mine, forever and ever. To wake up beside you in my big rice bed. To make babies together, wonderful, beautiful babies. To eat your lumpless oatmeal on cold winter mornings, because McNeills always eat oatmeal in the winter. Ah, Maura, I love you." And he kissed her in a way that left no doubt in her heart that he meant it.

"The woman you were with last night. The blonde," she said, trying to comprehend it all.

"I took her home right after dinner and rushed back to your house to wait for you. But you never arrived. By the way, something arrived. Mehitabel is now the proud mother of four kittens."

"You mean she didn't mean anything to you? She's not one of your—"

"Who? Mehitabel? I barely know her." His eyes were twinkling down at her.

"Don't be funny, Xan. I'm serious. The blonde in the restaurant."

"She was a blind date. A very lovely lady, but she's not you. Weren't you paying attention? I love you. *You.*"

She was filled with the happiness that came with being held in Xan's arms, and overlying that was the stirring, deep within her, of her hungering passion for him. She knew instinctively that her life was just about to begin, now, with Xan. It was the beginning that she would cherish most of all. "And I love you," she said, sure of him and sure of herself for the first time in a long, long time.

"Then your answer is yes?" he said, his lips brushing her cheek as he spoke.

"Yes," she said, and then after he kissed her again, a long sigh, "Yes."

And finally, joyously, with a knowledge so sure and so deep, Maura knew she had found, in Xan Copeland's arms, the world she was meant to know and the woman she was meant to be.

Epilogue

One Year Later

"Bear down, Maura," said Golden.

Maura gasped at the force of the pressure. Never mind how many birthings she had attended; it was different when it was your own baby being born. She gripped Golden's hand and, when the contraction was over, lifted her head to smile at her husband. She lay supported in his arms, half sitting, half lying between his thighs, in what she had found was the most comfortable position for her in her labor. Xan kissed her tenderly on the temple and worked a hand around to her swollen abdomen, massaging gently.

"Want some ice chips for your tongue?" Golden asked.

"Mmm, yes," said Maura drowsily. In between contractions she felt so sleepy, even though she'd only been in labor for five hours.

Golden moved swiftly to the kitchen area of the

birthing room. Every birthing room at Quinby Hospital was equipped not only with a kitchen where simple meals could be prepared but with its own bathroom. The birthing bed was covered with percale sheets in pastel colors.

In the privacy provided by Golden's temporary absence, Xan whispered in Maura's ear. "Comfortable?"

"I'd like more support for the small of my back," Maura told him. Xan maneuvered the pillows until Maura sighed in relief. "That's better," she murmured, lacing her fingers through his and bringing their entwined fingers to rest on one rounded breast. She had long ago shed the confining hospital gown, and she lay naked in his arms.

"I can feel your heart beating, strong and sure," Xan told her.

And then the next contraction came, and his eyes held hers, and Maura drew strength from their message of love. In this first year of their marriage, she had never felt closer or more connected to her husband than she did now, as they waited for their child to be born.

What a wonderful year it had been! Maura's practice had grown to embrace women who wanted home births in the most elegant homes on Teoway Island as well as in the most modest of homes in Shuffletown. She and Xan had combined their practices, had developed a working rapport that was fulfilling for both of them. Although they both now lived in Xan's house, Maura continued to work at McNeill Birth Center every day, and Xan kept his regular office hours. When Xan had been put in charge of the new birthing rooms at Quinby Hospital by an ailing Dr. Lyles, Maura had guided Xan toward making the hospital birthing rooms practical, comfortable and homey. It seemed only right that, since they had both worked so hard to make the Quinby Hospital birthing rooms a reality, their own child be born at Quinby with Golden's help.

Golden returned quickly and, waiting until a contraction had passed, placed slivers of ice on Maura's tongue. Maura closed her eyes until the next contraction overtook her.

"Maura, push, that's right, oh, your baby's head is crowning!" Golden sounded excited, happy.

Panting, Maura lifted her head and watched Golden over the mound of her abdomen. No, not her abdomen, her *baby*, her and Xan's *baby*, and the thought gave her strength so that her next push was a strong one.

"Let me lie back," she gasped, and instantly Xan slid from beneath her and moved around to where Golden was sitting between Maura's upraised legs. Now Maura could see him better, and she focused mightily on the love she felt for Xan. For this was the utmost expression of her love for this man, bearing his child.

And with beautiful harmony it happened: Maura felt their baby's body passing through hers, first the head, and then with another powerful effort that took all of Maura's strength, the baby itself slipping into

Xan's waiting hands, and in the joy of that perfect moment the three of them were irrevocably bonded into a family.

And Xan placed the baby gently, reverently, upon Maura's abdomen while Golden did what she had to do, and when Maura lifted her eyes to those of her husband, she was touched to see tears of love and pride and happiness shimmering in their green depths.

And there were joyful tears in Maura's eyes, too, and they slid unimpeded down her cheeks.

"A girl," said Xan, his voice breaking. "A beautiful, perfect baby girl." The baby began to cry, gathering air into her lungs, and Maura's heart gladdened at the sound.

With both hands she reached for her daughter, but she was exhausted from the effort of childbirth. Xan helped her to draw their baby to her full breast, where the sweet pink mouth groped for and finally found Maura's nipple.

Xan eased himself onto the side of the bed, marveling at the miracle. For it was a miracle. Maura had made him first perceive birth as a miracle long ago, back in Annie Bodkin's shack. But now he knew what the real miracle was. Not birth, not sexual contact between a man and a woman, but love. Love was the miracle, perhaps the only miracle that still existed in this crazy world.

Gently he lay down on the bed beside his wife and his child, thinking that he had never seen Maura looking more beautiful than she looked now. He would never forget the way she had looked with the sun shining through her ruby-red hair as she delivered Annie Bodkin's baby. Nor would he forget the glow in her eyes the first morning she'd ever awakened beside him in his big rice bed. Xan would always remember Maura as a lovely bride, swaying gracefully toward him down the aisle of the quaint little Teoway Island church. But today Maura was radiant, and her beauty transcended mere physical attributes.

Xan and Maura had worked side by side for several months, now that Maura had delivery-room and emergency-room privileges at Quinby Hospital, and there had been many times when he thanked whatever providence had sent her his way. But this lovingly achieved moment was the pinnacle of their relationship, and Xan exulted in it. It moved him immeasurably that this new human being, this tiny scrap of potential, his daughter, existed because of his love for this woman, his wife, his Maura, his love.

Maura, adjusting to the entirely new sensation of her baby's mouth tugging at her breast, could barely take her eyes off her child. Their new daughter was a pretty baby with a damp tuft of dark hair, long curly eyelashes and a healthy sucking reflex.

Maura leaned her head toward Xan, longing to rub her tear-streaked face against the comforting warmth of his cheek. Xan looked at her with so much joy and love and, yes, ecstasy that instead she lifted her lips to his.

They kissed, and she wanted to tell him that she had never before known how sexuality and spirituality could meld into one entity. She wanted to tell him that he had made her calling as a midwife more clear to her by his emotional involvement in the birth process. She wanted to tell him how much she appreciated his sensitivity and perception and caring. And she wanted to tell him how much she loved him, only she knew that there was no measure to describe it.

And so they kissed lingeringly, encompassing their child in their love, and the kiss was their past and their future, and it was their present.

For now, their kiss said it all. They had their whole lifetimes ahead of them to say the rest.

Harlequin

The Winds of Winter
Sandra Field

Harlequin Romance

Tender, captivating stories
that sweep to faraway
places and delight with the
magic of love.

Harlequin Presents...
VIOLET WINSPEAR
time of the temptress

Exciting romance novels
for the woman of today—
rare blend of passion and
dramatic realism.

Sensual and romantic
stories about choices,
dilemmas, resolutions, and
above all, the fulfillment
of love.

Harlequin Temptation
First Impressions
MARIS SOULE

GEN-A-2

Harlequin
is romance...

Share the joys and sorrows of real-life love with
Harlequin American Romance!™

GET THIS BOOK FREE as your introduction to Harlequin American Romance — an exciting series of romance novels written especially for the American woman of today.

Mail to:
Harlequin Reader Service

In the U.S.
2504 West Southern Ave.
Tempe, AZ 85282

In Canada
P.O. Box 2800, Postal Station A
5170 Yonge St., Willowdale, Ont. M2N 6J3

YES! I want to be one of the first to discover **Harlequin American Romance.** Send me FREE and without obligation *Twice in a Lifetime.* If you do not hear from me after I have examined my FREE book, please send me the 4 new **Harlequin American Romances** each month as soon as they come off the presses. I understand that I will be billed only $2.25 for each book (total $9.00). There are no shipping or handling charges. There is no minimum number of books that I have to purchase. In fact, I may cancel this arrangement at any time. *Twice in a Lifetime* is mine to keep as a FREE gift, even if I do not buy any additional books.

154-BPA-NAZJ

Name _____ (please print)

Address _____ Apt. no. _____

City _____ State/Prov. _____ Zip/Postal Code _____

Signature (If under 18, parent or guardian must sign.)

This offer is limited to one order per household and not valid to current Harlequin American Romance subscribers. We reserve the right to exercise discretion in granting membership. If price changes are necessary, you will be notified.